"He just a...
meant to k... ...

Wade's gut clenched at the way Aaliyah stared up at him with both disbelief and question. The assailant must think Aaliyah could identify him from the grave incident earlier that morning. Why else would he have risked such exposure twice more in the same day? There was a desperation to the action and a compulsion to be rid of Aaliyah that left Wade not only concerned but extremely suspicious...

"Do you think this is personal?" Wade ventured aloud.

Aaliyah stared at him. "Why? Do you?" she countered.

Wade's eyes caught a glimpse of something on the floor by her feet. He bent to retrieve it. The black woven thread of a bracelet with an arrowhead charm was encased in a plastic baggie. His hand closed around it as if by capturing the killer's calling card, he could capture the killer.

His eyes met Aaliyah's, and he answered her with honesty and not a little question in his voice. "Yeah. Yeah, I do think it's personal."

Jaime Jo Wright is an ECPA bestselling author and multi-award winner—including the Christy and Daphne du Maurier Awards. She is coffee-fueled and a cat-fancier extraordinaire and resides in Wisconsin's rural woodlands. Her literary vocation involves penning chilling tales, with a strong preference to the master of dark, Edgar Allan Poe. Visit her at jaimewrightbooks.com and listen to her podcast, *MadLit Musings*, on YouTube or your favorite podcast player.

Books by Jaime Jo Wright

Love Inspired Suspense

Buried Wilderness Secrets

Visit the Author Profile page at LoveInspired.com.

BURIED WILDERNESS SECRETS

JAIME JO WRIGHT

LOVE INSPIRED SUSPENSE
INSPIRATIONAL ROMANCE

LOVE INSPIRED® SUSPENSE
INSPIRATIONAL ROMANCE

Recycling programs
for this product may
not exist in your area.

ISBN-13: 978-1-335-95720-7

Buried Wilderness Secrets

Love Inspired
22 Adelaide St. West, 41st Floor
Toronto, Ontario M5H 4E3, Canada
www.LoveInspired.com

Printed in Lithuania

MIX
Paper | Supporting
responsible forestry
FSC® C021394

Can a woman forget her sucking child, that she should not have compassion on the son of her womb? yea, they may forget, yet will I not forget thee. Behold, I have graven thee upon the palms of my hands; thy walls are continually before me.
—*Isaiah* 49:15–16

To Jessica R. Patch, who said I could, so I did.

ONE

She wasn't supposed to find human bones in the wilderness.

Aaliyah Terrence gingerly toed the bone her dog had dropped at her feet before snatching her foot back in realization. Any other bone and she would have immediately questioned if it belonged to a deer, sheep or another form of animal ravaged by a bear or other predator. But she couldn't argue with the empty eye sockets staring back at her from the skull. The back half was broken off and missing, but the front gaped at her with the vacant stare that came with death and decay.

Aaliyah scanned the distance of the Montana wilderness, the shadows of the aspen and junipers suddenly more ominous than beautiful. She'd been called out as a park ranger to check the area. There had been reports of grizzlies messing with campers' tents. Probably more inexperienced outdoor enthusiasts who didn't know enough to store their food away from their campsites. But this? This was not expected.

"Where did you find this, Peaches?" Her words sounded loud in the natural stillness of the hills. Her black Labrador panted beside her, staring up at her with liquid brown eyes that were proud of her gift to Aaliyah. In spite of her horror, Aaliyah reached out to give Peaches a loving scratch of the ears. Peaches was the constant in her life. Aaliyah had rescued her black Lab from a shelter four years ago. The unconditional love of the dog healed some of those broken places inside of her. The ones that made Aaliyah question why her birth mother had ever given her up for adoption as a baby and doubt whether her adoptive parents could ever fill that hole inside of her.

Peaches shook her head, and her black ears flopped against her face. Aaliyah crouched in front of her dog, cupping the furry face between both palms.

A rising fear clenched her gut. She refused to allow her emotions to overtake her reason, and she eyed the skull with trepidation. "Where did you find this?" She scratched behind Peaches's ears. "Huh?"

Peaches dropped on her haunches, her tongue lolling from her muzzle. No answer was forthcoming—as Aaliyah expected. She snapped her finger at the dog, and Peaches jumped to her feet. "Show me." Aaliyah's command earned her a dog smile and short bark. "Show me, girl," Aaliyah encouraged, and Peaches started off deeper into the lodgepole pine forest.

The landscape took on a sinister appearance now, and Aaliyah resisted it. But the skull she left paces behind on the ground taunted her innate love for the wilderness region of the Bob Marshall. Peaches paused and looked over her shoulder at Aaliyah as if to inquire if Aaliyah was following. "Good girl," Aaliyah crooned. "I'm coming."

Not too much farther back into the trees, Aaliyah saw ground that was disturbed. Earth had been turned over and appeared to have been tamped down again. Flattened, with some random brush strewn over it like camouflage. She lifted her eyes to survey the area, and a few yards to the east, Aaliyah saw more earth, but this time in haphazard piles where Peaches had been digging.

She carefully edged her way toward the spot, watching her step—although uncertain what she was watching for and not willing to let her mind pose the questions that she was barely keeping at bay.

Peaches bounded ahead and was distracted by the scent of something new. Aaliyah let her go as she approached Peaches's dig spot. Aaliyah sucked in a breath as she caught glimpses of gray bone peeking from beneath the dirt. What appeared to be bony fingertips poked from the grave, and Aaliyah blinked rapidly against a sudden feeling of panic.

Get it together, Terrence. Her mental coaching and measured breaths calmed her, and Aaliyah turned to eye flattened earth behind her.

Another grave?

Was this a burial ground of sorts?

Or worse—a killer's burial ground?

A glimmer of reflected sunlight by the disturbed ground caught her attention. Aaliyah moved toward it, crouching down as she saw a metal object half hidden in scrub brush. Being extra cautious, Aaliyah bent even closer to the earth, unwilling to reach out and move it until she knew what it was.

The chain link gold of a bracelet met her eyes; a finely etched silver arrowhead connected it. It was thick, manly, and assuming the metals were authentic, not at all inexpensive. Arrowhead jewelry wasn't an anomaly in the Western states, by any means, but something of this apparent quality also wasn't typically found deep in the wilderness near what appeared to be a grave.

Aaliyah sat back on her heels.

She needed to call this in. The satellite phone she carried

with her would be the answer over her cell phone, which wouldn't have a signal until she'd gone down in elevation. Aaliyah moved to retrieve it from her waist clip, but she heard a stick snap from somewhere in the woods, and her hand froze, hovering over the phone.

Aaliyah twisted, staring into the trees. Peaches had stilled in her place deeper in the woods, her nose tilted upward, the hackles on her black fur raised. A low growl vibrated in her throat. The feeling that Aaliyah was not alone assaulted her, and she scrambled to release the phone so she could call for help. It was against the odds she would run into anyone, but perhaps it was the campers who'd reported the grizzly activity earlier that morning. And yet—Aaliyah's gaze dropped back to the precious metal bracelet and its arrowhead—there was motivation a killer would return to retrieve that. Value aside, it was evidence. If these were graves, that meant that someone had not only dug them, but filled them with the bodies, one of which Peaches had just dug up.

She grappled for the phone, her hand closing around its thick body. Help was needed, but it wouldn't come quickly. Not here in the wilderness. The nearest ranger station was miles away, and the roads into the Bob Marshall Wilderness were narrow, rutted and gravel.

Aaliyah stilled again.

A breeze lifted the hair along her neck like fingers trailing across her skin.

Peaches growled and then stilled.

Another stick snapped, and this time it was directly behind her. Aaliyah spun, but her movement was put to an abrupt end as she caught sight of a pistol in her peripheral vision. An arm swung it against Aaliyah's temple, and sharp pain reverberated through her head as her neck snapped to the side. She slumped to the ground, desperate to catch a glimpse of the person who had snuck up behind her. But all Aaliyah saw as the blackness crowded her vision was an arm reaching down and a hand curling around the bracelet.

The killer had returned for it.

Aaliyah was the unfortunate interruption.

She heard a sharp bark, and her world went dark.

Her head throbbed, and Aaliyah struggled to open her eyes. The world swam before her, and it took a moment to regain her senses. The trees towered over her like sentinels where she lay on the ground. Peaches licked her neck and the blood that trailed down her face from the wound on the side of her head.

The graves!

Recollection flooded over her, and Aaliyah moved to sit up suddenly, but the woods spun around her, and she lay back down with a groan. The grass and sticks beneath her body crunched as she rolled to her side. Peaches whined, nudging Aaliyah with her cold nose.

"I'm—fine," Aaliyah croaked out for her dog's concerned benefit. But she wasn't. She'd been pistol-whipped, and she had no idea how long she'd been out. She maneuvered to her knees, blinking rapidly to clear her vision.

The killer had left her for dead. Or maybe Peaches had intercepted him?

Aaliyah darted a look at the shrubbery. The bracelet was gone.

She fumbled for the satellite phone hooked to her belt. Within seconds, a voice pierced the airways, its familiarity a comfort considering the circumstances. But Aaliyah wasn't convinced she was out of danger, and she did her best to scan her surroundings in spite of the throbbing wound at her temple.

"What's up, Terrence?" Gordon Halstead, a fellow ranger and a trusted friend, answered her call. "I'm at the station. You coming in for the day?"

"Gordon, I need you to—" Aaliyah paused to control the quivering in her voice.

"Something wrong?" Gordon's tone changed to one of concern, his voice clear as he responded on his own sat phone.

Aaliyah could imagine the look in his green eyes. He had at least twenty-some years on her, and at times she would rely on him to help steady her. The time the missing hikers hadn't been found until twenty-nine hours later—it'd been Gordon who'd encouraged Aaliyah to keep pressing on. They'd find them. And they had. She needed that Gordon-style confidence now. She loved her career as a ranger. The Montana Bob Marshall Wilderness was her home—it was her safe place. Until now.

"Aaliyah?"

Realizing she still hadn't answered him, she swallowed hard. "I'm going to need you to call the authorities." Aaliyah closed her eyes as a wave of pain swept over her head.

"We *are* the authorities out here." He gave a short laugh.

Aaliyah shook her head, even though Gordon couldn't see her. "No. This is beyond us. I found graves. Someone attacked me."

"Attacked you? What kind of graves? *Human* graves?" Gordon's questions fired at her as if from a gun. "Are you all right? Aaliyah?"

"The graves are human," Aaliyah managed to get out. "Peaches found a human skull, and then when I investigated— Gordon, there are at least two graves here." Nausea swelled in her throat.

Gordon's stern voice pulled her back into the conversation. "Are you sure they're *human*?"

"It's impossible to mistake the skull as anything else. And—at least the one grave has more remains in it. I saw it before I was hit over the head with a gun." Aaliyah tugged off the bandana she wore around her neck and tied it to a nearby log for a marker, all while she hugged the phone between her shoulder and ear. "I'm marking the spot, then I'm getting out of here."

"Are you okay to get back alone?" Concern etched her partner's voice.

"I don't have a choice," Aaliyah admitted. "I want to get out of here. Can you call the authorities?"

"On it," was Gordon's reply.

The police station buzzed with activity when Wade Marlowe strode in. A few hours' drive from Helena and he was ready to stretch his legs and locate some coffee. But he needed to connect with Sheriff Buck Halstead first, although—Wade scanned the station—the amount of hustle right now was concerning. A phone rang. Two cops brushed by him, leaving behind the distinct smell of burned coffee. Yeah, he needed coffee.

"Can I help you?" The female attendant behind the desk and plexiglass gave him a harried look.

Wade flipped open his badge so she could read it. "Detective Wade Marlowe, from the Helena Police Department. I'm here to meet with the sheriff."

The middle-aged woman pursed her lips and widened her eyes. "Get in line, Detective. This place is seeing more action today than it has in twenty years."

"What's going on?" Wade leaned against the counter.

"Had a body called in from the Bob," she said, using

the local nickname for the Bob Marshall Wilderness. "A ranger and her dog came across a human skull this morning, and her partner called us in."

"Is it fresh?"

She glanced over her shoulder as one cop shouted to another and tossed him a set of keys. Redirecting her attention back to Wade, she muttered, "I'll let the sheriff fill you in."

Wade could read between the lines. This wasn't his jurisdiction, so really none of his business, and she certainly wasn't going to be at fault for discussing something she wasn't supposed to.

"Marlowe!" Sheriff Halstead's booming voice drew both their attention as he entered the room. Apparently, he remembered Wade from past meetings. It made the moment less complicated to do away with reintroductions. "Better get your hustle on. You're going to want to come with me." He motioned for Wade to follow. Within seconds, they were striding toward the back door. "Good to see you. It's been a few years."

"Good to see you too, Sheriff," Wade exchanged pleasantries.

"Buck. Call me Buck. Everyone does!" The sheriff made small talk without explaining where they were going.

An SUV waited for them in the parking lot.

"Get in." Buck directed Wade, who, with a longing look back at the station and the potential hope of burned coffee, acquiesced.

He buckled his seat belt as he settled into the passenger seat.

Buck slid beside him. "You heard about the skull?"

"Yeah. What's going on?"

The sheriff backed out of the parking space. "Good friends of mine—their daughter, Aaliyah Terrence, is my goddaughter. She also works as a ranger, and her dog came up with a human skull this morning. Then she was attacked."

"Attacked?" Wade's body tensed.

Buck offered a grim smile as he steered his vehicle. "It sounds like the perp left a bracelet behind. He must've come back for it and found Aaliyah. My brother, Gordon, actually works with her, and he called me. I got a team out there to meet up with Aaliyah. They've discovered two graves, possibly a third. One of them is fairly recent. But the one with the skull? It's significantly older." His sideways glance at Wade made the hair at the back of Wade's neck stand up and little bumps rise on the skin of his arms.

"Are you saying that—"

"The graves aren't far from where the cold case started from twenty-five years ago. The one that you just called me about."

Wade didn't answer. He was at a loss for words as he chewed over the added information. He'd been a cold case detective out of Helena, Montana, for several years now, but this case—this case had gnawed at him the moment he'd seen the crime scene photos. Twenty-five years ago, a young woman had been murdered in the Bob Marshall Wilderness. She'd been found by a park ranger then, not unlike today's circumstances.

"Has the body been identified—the skull?" Wade broke from his musing about his own case that he'd come to Park Springs to piece together.

Buck gave a small snort. "Not yet. It's just bones. There doesn't appear to be anything left to identify it with on sight."

"And there are two other graves?" Wade had to reconfirm. This could change his entire investigation if it was linked to his cold case.

"Could be. We don't know for certain. The area is being cordoned off as we speak. I'm guessing other branches of enforcement will be here in no time. I can't help but wonder…"

Wade filled in the missing blanks. "If it's related to Deborah Platt?"

The sheriff's lips thinned as he pressed them together. He gripped the steering wheel tighter, his knuckles whitening. "Now that you know who your cold case victim is…you may have just earned yourself a few more to figure out."

This wasn't the outcome Wade had hoped for.

A brown-headed cowbird chortled overhead, sounding like a mix of a pinball machine and a video game from the arcade. Aaliyah struggled to find solid footing in the scree along the base of the larger cliff that rose to her left. Despite her hiking boots, the loose bits of broken rock gave way beneath her weight like sand on the shore. Adjusting her position, Aaliyah scrambled upward toward the base of the cliff, the vast expanse of wilderness hidden by the height of Ponderosa pines and poplars.

Her head throbbed, and she questioned her reasoning power even as she pushed forward. *Peaches*. Her dog always listened—always obeyed. Now, with dusk settling in, the site being cordoned off and law enforcement taking over, Aaliyah had noticed that Peaches was not in her usual spot in the cab of the truck. The last thing Aaliyah needed was her dog interfering with the investigation.

Taking off to find Peaches was potentially foolhardy, but law enforcement had reiterated that whoever had attacked her was long gone. There was no evidence left behind, no indication that there was anyone in the area; there weren't even ATV tracks. How the perpetrator had even gotten to the graves was a mystery.

Now Aaliyah looked for her dog's prints and followed them, willing away her headache, thankful the medic had ruled out a concussion. She loved the lurking shadows of the forest, the crystal blue hues of the Flathead River, the occasional grizzly or wolf sighting. But never had the wilderness been a place of terror for her. The can of bear spray hooked to her ranger's belt slammed into a boulder. She clambered around to the back side of the boulder and was relieved to see the unsteady ground was leveling and patches of earth provided sturdier footing. She was climbing upward. Toward the shelter of the trees, the hovering angles of the cliff above her. The cave areas had to be only a quarter of a mile away from where Peaches had found the bone.

Where *had* Peaches taken off to?

She reassured herself she was doing the right thing looking for Peaches as she scrambled into the covering of the trees. She'd lost her ranger's flat hat, and her head felt not only barren, but also like a beacon of light giving away her position. That was what she got for having red hair.

A bullet ricocheted off the cliff right above her, sending limestone shards raining down onto her head. She scurried under the cover of a scrub bush. Aaliyah tried to control her breathing as she crawled along the rocky earth. Her palms stung as her skin scraped against the rough terrain.

Aaliyah pulled her body around the edge of the embankment, rolling from her stomach onto her backside. Her trousers were torn at the knee, and blood was seeping into the material. She'd landed on a root jutting up from the ground. The bank behind her was thick with shrub and trees, but the undergrowth was thin and manageable. If she could get lost in there, she'd be difficult to spot until she could find the cave and take cover, and then—

A hand clamped around her upper arm, yanking her backward.

Aaliyah's scream was cut short as another hand cupped her mouth, pressing her head back into a firm chest.

"Shhh!"

The whisper was gravelly and unfamiliar. Aaliyah thrashed to escape. How her assailant had found his way from below her and within shooting distance to now behind her was a riddle she hadn't time to solve.

"Lemme—goff—" Aaliyah struggled against the man's grip, twisting her head back and forth to free her mouth from his persistent hold.

"I said *be quiet*! You're going to get us shot!"

The words stilled her for a moment, which seemed to be enough for the man holding her to trust her. He loosened his grip and hauled her backward, farther into the shelter of the trees and the sloping landscape.

Aaliyah fell away from him, ready to claw his face if necessary. Her bear spray slapped against her hip, and she fumbled to release it from its holster. It would easily blind a man. Easily—

"Don't move."

The command made her freeze. Aaliyah lifted her eyes to meet the steady mahogany-brown gaze of a man who was not at all the way she pictured a mountain-man killer. His dark jeans encased strong limbs. His navy blue T-shirt peeked out from beneath a gray Oxford shirt that was now dusty from their wrestling. He wore practical boots and had a sidearm holstered on his left side. He was a lefty. That was unusual.

"Any movement could expose us." He held up both his palms to appease her uncertainty.

"Who are you?" Aaliyah demanded.

"Marlowe. Detective Wade Marlowe, out of Helena."

"Detective?" She didn't believe him.

He didn't try to hide his look of exasperation as he dug into his pocket for his badge. After he flashed it at her, Aaliyah wasn't sure if she was relieved or more confused.

"You don't believe me." The far too good-looking detective tucked his badge away. When he raised his eyes to hers again, they were matter-of-fact. He hadn't taken her questions or doubts personally. "I saw you wandering off from the site. Not a smart move. Still, we need to get—"

Another bullet *zinged* past them.

Detective Marlowe was flung backward, and he grabbed at his right arm.

Aaliyah scurried to his side. With his good arm, the detective pulled her toward him so they could keep climbing, grasping her hand with a grip that was anything but warm and kind. It was urgent. It was the type of grip you didn't let go of, for fear if you did, your life would be over.

TWO

Wade noted the tremble in Aaliyah Terrence's hand, but he couldn't stop to offer comfort now. It *had* to be Aaliyah Terrence—the one Buck had told him about who'd discovered the skull. The one Wade had *not* told the sheriff he had driven all the way from Helena to find. There hadn't been time.

Okay, that wasn't true. There had been time, but the pressure of the discovery of another body—and more victims—far outweighed any urgency in a twenty-five-year-old cold case. But then Halstead had mentioned the ranger's name. Aaliyah Terrence. And she was Buck's goddaughter? Irony was too much of a friend these days. Of course it'd be her, of course he would be the one to see her venture from the cordoned-off area for whatever reason, and of course it was his own penchant to protect people that had made him follow her. Now it'd gotten him shot.

"There's a cave—" Aaliyah gasped as she struggled to keep up with him. "About an eighth of a mile northwest."

Wade tossed her a look. He could see the wound on her head, bandaged now but still red at the edges. The woman had taken a pistol whip and was still out here investigating. He didn't know if he should be impressed or irritated at her reckless actions.

"What are you doing out here anyway?" he asked under his breath. He would need first aid on the bullet graze soon, but it wasn't life threatening, so for now, they needed to keep moving.

"Looking for my dog."

Her dog. Of course. A dog was not unlike a child, and a mother would do anything for it. Still, Wade eyed Aaliyah Terrence. Her flaming red hair was a drawback since someone with a gun was chasing them, yet he couldn't help but notice it glimmered with flecks of gold and highlighted the golden glitter in her hazel eyes. She was pretty. She wasn't what he'd expected. His twenty-five-year-old cold case had him picturing Aaliyah Terrence to be older. Not the age his sister was—*should* be. The memory of Amy skewered him with a throb that matched that of his right arm from the bullet. He could feel his sleeve becoming sticky with blood.

"There. The cave is that way!" Aaliyah pointed up the craggy cliffside.

Wade shook his head. "No cave. It'll leave us cornered. It's obvious whoever is out there knows this territory as well as you do. The last thing we need is to be trapped with no way out."

They hadn't stopped hiking at a breakneck pace. Thankfully the ground was solid now, and they were getting deeper into the trees and covering. They were within half a mile of the graves—Wade knew the authorities at the site would have heard the shots too. Help should be on its way.

"What do you suggest we do?"

It was an honest question, and Wade had to give the woman credit. A lot of people would have been huddled on the ground having a panic attack. Instead, Aaliyah showed grit, even though her face was white.

"We head back. To where the investigation is going on.

The more people, the less likely an attack is. Unless the guy is a complete lunatic."

"He's a killer—he has to be a lunatic."

Wade snorted at the sarcasm in Aaliyah's voice. "Yeah, well—apparently he didn't do a good enough job with you."

Aaliyah drew back, skewering him with her golden gaze.

Ouch. That had been the wrong choice of words. Wade tried to correct himself. "I meant, you're blessed the guy didn't actually do you in when he hit you."

Aaliyah's expression softened a bit. "I think my dog might have scared him away. I heard her bark before I blacked out." Her face blanched. "He would have killed me."

"Well, let's not stick around to give him more of a second chance." Wade gripped her hand for no other reason than to urge her along and keep her close in case protection was needed.

The next several minutes were tense, as they moved as fast as they could while trying to stay under the cover of the trees. Wade was never so grateful as when he spotted some of the team through the undergrowth, and of course, there next to the team was a black Labrador.

"Peaches!" Aaliyah's breath of relief was a momentary distraction.

Wade shot her a look and then called out, "Ho!" He avoided waving his injured arm. "There's an armed assailant running loose. We need to pull teams back and clear the area."

The officer who responded indicated the activity behind him. "We heard it. We're pulling back now. They've dispatched a team to track the shooter down."

Wade doubted they'd find anyone, especially if he was right and the shooter knew the terrain.

Hiking to the main tent and the law enforcement vehicles parked beside it, Wade motioned for Aaliyah to follow him.

"You're bleeding." A strident voice sliced the air. An older woman with chin-length gray hair assessed him. Wade read her tag. *Detective Jenson.*

Jenson eyed Aaliyah. "Are you all right?"

"I'm fine." Aaliyah sounded breathless.

"Good." Jenson clicked her tongue and motioned to Wade. "Get over here so we can treat that arm."

"There's an assailant—"

"We know." Jenson interrupted Wade, and he bit his tongue to keep from retorting to the sharp woman who meant well but seemed to lack social skills. "We heard the shots. The team has stopped searching the grounds for now until the area is cleared."

"Did you find any more—" Aaliyah clipped her words.

She was standing close to him. Probably closer than she realized. He could feel the heat from the skin of her arm, which almost brushed his and—nope. Wade shut that part of his mind off. He wasn't the type of guy any woman could be safe with. Not after Amy—not after he'd let his sister die.

"Bodies?" Jenson grunted at Aaliyah, finishing her question for her. Jenson's face gave nothing away as she ripped Wade's shirt sleeve to reveal his bloodied and bullet-grazed bicep.

"Two more," she answered, her nose inches away from his arm. "So far."

"Four total," Wade surmised. The sinking feeling in his gut did nothing to assuage the hope he also felt. Hope that he might be able to close more than one cold case this time. That he might be able to give other families the closure he'd never had.

"Four is only the beginning, I'm afraid." Jenson's voice

softened in apparent respect for the victims. "I think it's a dumping ground. Plain and simple. And you, young lady—" she shot a glance at Aaliyah "—have made its owner a very unhappy man."

Buck gave Aaliyah a look from beneath his peppered-black eyebrows, which resembled caterpillars growing fur for the winter. "That was a foolish thing to do, kid."

Aaliyah was used to her godfather's gruff censure. She'd grown up around it, Buck being such good friends with her dad and spending a lot of his free time at her parents' ranch. He was a crusty old bachelor—just like her coworker and his brother, Gordon—and they were both like the uncles she'd never had. Now, and understandably so, Buck was not happy that she'd gone after Peaches. Especially when Peaches ended up back at her truck of her own free will, and Aaliyah only had a wounded detective to show for it.

Detective Wade Marlowe seemed no worse for the wear as he lounged in a hard chair at the police station. His arm was bandaged. He'd refused to go to the hospital, just like she had. Now he held a cup of coffee with a look on his square-jawed face that said the only medicine he needed was the black brew before him.

"Never risk your life for an animal's," Buck insisted.

Aaliyah shifted her gaze to the badge pinned to his shirt, then his eyes. They were narrowed in seriousness.

"I don't care if it *is* Peaches," he finished.

"I wasn't worried about Peaches," Aaliyah lied, her bottom resting on the edge of the sheriff's desk. A phone with its spiral cord sat on the corner. There was a desk lamp and a box of facial tissues. She reached for one and made pretense of casually wiping her nose, but she was concerned the two men might notice the tremor in her fingers. "I didn't want my dog interfering with the crime scene."

Buck *harrumphed* with conviction, knowing full well that Aaliyah would do anything just shy of illegal and immoral to keep Peaches safe and unharmed.

Wade slurped his coffee and then rested his chocolate-eyed gaze on her. "At any point, did you catch a look at your attacker?"

Aaliyah tossed the wadded-up tissue into the wastebasket at the side of the desk. Wade was staring at her as though she were about to recite a full description of their would-be killer.

"No." She shook her head, conscious that her red hair was wisping out in frizzy directions. "I didn't see anyone. I mean, not really."

"What do you mean 'not really'?" Buck inserted.

"I mean, I could tell it was a man. I saw his arm when he reached for the bracelet, and then I passed out."

"What identifiers *could* you see on his arm?" Wade coaxed.

"I don't know." Aaliyah shrugged, frustration mounting for not knowing and irritation growing toward both men before her—one familiar and one a stranger—who seemed to think she should be offering them a lot more information. "He was Caucasian—I think. That's all I know."

"And this bracelet you saw—he took it?" Wade concluded.

"He must have. It wasn't there when I came to. But I *did* see it. It was gold and silver, and it looked expensive," Aaliyah concluded. She turned back to Buck. "Did you want me to draw a sketch of it?"

Buck nodded. "Of course. If you can."

"And you're sure it was a man's bracelet?" Wade verified.

"Yes." Aaliyah nodded and then grimaced, trying to ignore her headache. "Can I ask who you are exactly?" Aaliyah wanted to bite her tongue the moment the question escaped. She didn't mean to sound so suspicious of him—so rude. He'd pretty much saved her life. Literally had taken a bullet for her. But she also knew Buck. As sheriff, he didn't welcome outside law enforcement unless there was a good reason. He preferred to keep things local, to his force and his oversight. His ease with this detective who had inserted himself into the investigation was an irregularity.

Wade tipped his head toward his injured arm. "I'd offer to shake hands but—"

Aaliyah narrowed her eyes at the hint of sarcasm in his tone.

Wade ignored her censure. "You know my name already."

"And?" Aaliyah looked between him and Buck.

Buck had moved to a far counter boasting a coffeepot that was still flicked on per the glowing orange button and the scent of burning liquid. He spoke over his shoulder as he poured himself a mug. "And Detective Marlowe is here to investigate that cold case from years back."

"The unknown woman?" Aaliyah was as familiar with it as anyone from Park Springs. She'd grown up hearing stories of the murdered woman no one had been able to identify. "Why now?"

"The State of Montana wants to see cold cases closed. I was assigned this one."

"Well, have fun." Aaliyah offered a conciliatory smile. "No one's figured out anything about that case. Just lots of local lore and ghost stories."

Buck cleared his throat, and he handed Aaliyah her own cup of coffee as he approached her. She took it as he explained further. "Fact is, kid, Marlowe is here because they've figured out who the victim is."

"You're kidding." Aaliyah shot a startled look at Wade.

The detective slouched in his chair, his legs stretched out in front of him, but there was an increased tension in his face. A muscle twitched in his scruffy jaw. He avoided her eyes. "Yeah. Yeah, we ran her DNA through CODIS, the national database, and came up with a hit."

"Can I ask who she was?" Aaliyah was certain the answer would be no, so she was surprised when Wade's dark stare collided with hers as he announced it.

"The hit in the system was for a biological sister. Once we traced her, we were able to pinpoint the name of our victim as Deborah Platt."

Aaliyah heard the plastic clock on the wall ticking time in the ensuing silence. Wade Marlowe studied her so intently she grew uncomfortable. A glance at Buck told her the sheriff was waiting to hear more also.

"I've never heard of a Deborah Platt," Aaliyah finally stated to avoid the ongoing stillness.

"Never?" Wade raised an eyebrow.

"Should I have?" She shot Buck a desperate look. He shrugged as if he were as in the dark as she.

Wade pulled his legs up and drew in a deep breath. Releasing it, he gripped his mug of coffee like a doctor who was about to inform a family of a terminal diagnosis. He tapped the toe of his boot a few times and then cleared his throat. "The DNA I ran came back as a familial match for a Lori Racer—used to go by her family name of Platt. She was Deborah's younger sister. She'd spent some time in and out of the system for drugs."

Aaliyah waited. He was going somewhere with this, and the tightening in her stomach gave off warning signals.

Wade rubbed the back of his neck as he continued. "Lori confirmed Deborah's identity. Her sister had been missing for years, and facts all lined up. But she also let us know something we weren't expecting."

"Which was?" Aaliyah raised her eyebrow, a bit irritated at Wade's pauses.

"Lori's daughter had done one of those online genetic tests. She submitted her DNA to the records in case of unknown familial relations, and they recently got notified of a match. A pretty close match, if I'm honest. It was for someone who would be Lori's biological niece—her daughter's first cousin."

Aaliyah didn't want to acknowledge the dread that was forming inside of her. That premonition of knowing where this was going before she was told. That she, herself, had recently done a genetic test but was debating on connecting with the DNA hits she'd received.

"Lori's daughter is your cousin, Aaliyah. And the way the DNA points, Deborah Platt—our cold case victim— well…she's your mother."

The words froze her into a motionless stare.

She heard Buck exclaim under his breath.

There was no denying the expression of frank conviction on Wade Marlowe's face. He believed what he'd just declared with all his being. And apparently, he had DNA to back it up.

Wade watched the myriad of emotions flicker across Aaliyah Terrence's face. He felt like an absolute heel, but how else did someone break the news of a birth mother's identity to a person? Of course, her birth mother was not only dead, but also the subject of a cold case that was legendary in her hometown. Yeah, he probably should've taken care to couch his announcement more gently. Not to mention the pallor of Aaliyah's face made him worry that maybe she wasn't as "okay" as she'd claimed to be after the earlier attack.

"That's not true." Aaliyah shook her head and gave Sheriff Halstead a desperate look. "Buck, tell the detective that's a ludicrous statement."

Buck opened his mouth, then snapped it shut. He turned his coffee mug in his hands. "Aaliyah, I—" With a pointed look at Wade, the sheriff seemed to fumble for words.

Wade refused to feel guilty about the tears that glowed in Aaliyah's eyes. They were piercing, like Amy's. His sister had always had a way of getting to him when she cried, and he couldn't let Aaliyah Terrence do the same. He had a case to solve. He had a family to protect—Aaliyah and her newfound extended family, the Platts.

"It's DNA. It doesn't lie." He meant to explain more, but Aaliyah shoved herself off her perch on the metal desk.

"That's just…no. That's ridiculous." She shook her head, and the expression on her face was lost and bewildered. "Buck—tell him."

Buck coughed, his own face void of color. It was a connection that the sheriff had obviously not been prepared for either.

Wade stood slowly to meet her, noticing he was only a couple inches taller than she was. The vulnerability she couldn't hide struck him deeply. "I'm sorry to tell you this way, but I came up to Park Springs to investigate, and then after the happenings of today I'm wondering—"

"If it's connected to Deborah Platt's cold case?" Aaliyah crossed her arms over her chest and didn't bother to hide the tear that slipped down her cheek. "Detective Marlowe." Her voice trembled. "Are you trying to imply that not only have you identified the murdered woman from twenty-five years ago here in Park Springs, but you also think she's tied to the remains *my* dog discovered this morning, *and* she's my *birth mother*?"

Wade knew it was a lot. "I don't—"

Aaliyah swept her arm forward with a frustrated cry. Her hand connected with her full mug of coffee on the corner of the desk, and it flew onto the floor, spilling coffee on the tile. Buck leaped back from the splash. Wade took the coffee with full force to the front of his jeans. With a sucked-in sob, Aaliyah sprinted from the room and down the hall of the police station.

"Aaliyah!" Sheriff Halstead shouted after her.

Wade ignored the throbbing in his upper arm where the bullet had left its signature. He tossed the sheriff a firm "I'll go after her," and disregarded the sheriff when he told Wade to just let Aaliyah go.

Letting her go was the worst thing he could do. He'd let his sister go, and she died because of his decision. Trauma was nothing to bear alone. He'd learned that lesson the hard way.

Aaliyah choked back angry tears. It wasn't right, it wasn't fair, it wasn't true. The string of denials circled in her mind like a carousel stuck at high speed. So many people didn't understand the implications of being adopted. Yes, she had wonderful parents, Buck who was like an uncle, a beautiful place in which to grow up. But she always was aware of that empty space in her soul that asked questions about why she hadn't been worth keeping, and why it had been okay to give a child away, and who she was. That was *the* nagging question. Who was she?

Wade Marlowe seemed to think he knew.

She had been on a journey in taking the genetic test.

But shouldn't it have been on her time, when she wanted to connect to the DNA hits that showed she had relations in the world? She'd issued her impulsive "say it's not true" to Buck just a minute ago because this wasn't the outcome Aaliyah had dreamed of. A birth mother who was not only dead, but had been murdered? It was the worst possible end case scenario.

Aaliyah heard Wade shout behind her. Her first name even, as though they were old friends.

She stumbled to a halt on the sidewalk outside a quaint café with horseshoes and wildflowers painted on its window. Her truck was only a few parking spots away, but the thumping of Wade's shoes on the sidewalk told her he'd catch up to her before she made it there anyway.

He trotted up to her, drawing close and eyeing her with a pitying expression that she didn't like. His dark hair flopped over his forehead, and he shoved it back with his hand.

"Listen, I'm sorry it came out so blunt."

Aaliyah shook her head. "You think you have the facts." She swallowed the lump in her throat. "You don't."

"Then tell me the facts," he challenged softly.

Aaliyah waited as a woman passed them leading a floppy-eared mutt on a leash. A polite smile and nod of heads were exchanged, and then Aaliyah turned back to Wade.

"I was adopted as a baby. That's all I know. My parents said the adoption records were sealed by court order."

Wade appeared skeptical. "By the end of the nineties most adoptions were open."

"But not all adoptions." Aaliyah scowled.

"Fair enough." Wade shifted his weight to his other foot. "Still, the DNA evidence shows that—"

"No." Aaliyah put up her hand. "You haven't properly

investigated this." It was a flimsy argument; it was insult-
ing, and she saw it irked Wade.

His dark eyes flashed. "You can't do much more to prove
someone's identity than to match DNA. It's irrefutable."

Aaliyah swiped at her eyes, brushing the hot tears from
them. She waved him off. "Just—please, stop. It's too much
for today. Just too much." She choked on the words, grasping for breath and control.

Wade took a step toward her, concern etched into the
corners of his eyes.

Aaliyah stepped away from him. She drilled him with a
look that she hoped would impress on him all the emotion
she was warring against in this moment. "You're always
on that side of the fence, aren't you? Telling families their
loved one has been killed. It must be comforting to never
be on this side, Detective Marlowe, having to swallow a
truth you never wanted to hear. Murder is a vicious concept,
and you are far too careless with it. Just leave me alone."

Aaliyah ignored the way Wade's face paled, the way his
body stiffened and his chest heaved as he sucked in a deep
breath. Let him be offended! It was only fair. She half ran
the rest of the way to her truck, fingering the key fob in her
hand so she could drive away as fast as possible.

She ignored the stricken expression on his face as she
tugged the shifter into gear and backed from her parking
spot with a squeal of her tires. She needed to get home.
Gordon had left Peaches there for Aaliyah earlier, and now
she ached to bury her face in her dog's furry neck. Not to
mention, she needed to lie down. Today had been one she
wanted to forget.

Aaliyah turned the corner, glad to leave the sheriff's
office behind. The horror of the day left her shaken. She
reached for her water bottle jammed into the cupholder be-

tween her seat and the passenger side. As she did so, she caught sight of a foreign object on the seat.

"What—?"

A terrifying truth crept up her spine and sent chills down to her feet.

On the passenger seat lay one of the bracelets sold by the dozens at the local gas station. A black leather strip with a faux bone arrowhead dangling from it.

It wasn't her bracelet.

Aaliyah recalled she'd not locked her truck doors—she never did. Not in small town Park Springs, Montana.

But today? She should have. The killer had left her a message. He had returned for one bracelet that morning. He would return for this one—and for her. It was evident he believed she was a liability, and that maybe she could even identify him. But now he was toying with her also. Playing with her mind like a master pulled the strings on a puppet just before he cut them.

THREE

Wade checked the house number against the note on his phone. It matched. This little white ranch-style home with a grove of poplar trees was Aaliyah's. Buck had given him her address after warning Wade it was probably best if he left her alone. But that wasn't in his wheelhouse of gifts and talents.

His mind conjured up the last evening with Amy. Their argument. The way his sister had slammed the door to his apartment after fighting with him about her decision to not attend college. Hours later, she'd been found murdered and left on a trail in their local park. Wade's world was never the same. He should have followed Amy. Should have made sure she was okay and not allowed their argument to stand between them. Instead, he'd stewed about the disagreement and busied himself with stuff that he'd needed to get done, sure that he was correct and Amy was wrong.

That wouldn't happen tonight. Even if Aaliyah was no relation, even if she was a virtual stranger, Wade had vowed on Amy's memory that he wouldn't do that to anyone ever again. The sun would not go down on their wrath. He would make sure of it. Besides, he still had more questions—especially after the information Buck had offered to him an hour ago.

Wade slammed his car door shut and gave Aaliyah's yard a once over. With night settling in, the shadows were growing longer, the corners and edges of places darker. He reached up and touched his bandaged arm. He knew a bullet graze would heal quickly and without any lasting damage, but it still stung.

He didn't like the way Aaliyah's yard had hiding places. Bushes against the garage. An alcove by a small shed. Some decorative boulders at the corner of her lot. There were houses on both sides of hers with their own hiding places. Aaliyah needed to be safe tonight. There was no indication the shooter would try to find her, but then, there was no reason for them to have expected any of the events of today. The more worrisome fact was the risks the shooter had taken to attempt to silence Aaliyah, especially with the number of authorities already swarming his body dump site. That he'd wanted Aaliyah dead at the potential cost of his own exposure proved the killer was desperate. That fact ate at Wade. She'd either seen the shooter and didn't realize it, or the shooter believed she had. Or maybe he believed he could be identified based on the bracelet alone.

Wade strode up the sidewalk, glad to see she had her porch light on. Light streamed from the front windows too, even though she had curtains pulled. An unfamiliar noise from the west caught his attention. Wade paused on the steps, squinting into the setting sun. The rolling hills beyond were turning hues of purple tipped in orange. The neighboring home, much like Aaliyah's, had a deck that wrapped around the house, angles and levels providing even more places for a person to stay out of sight. Wade strained to see if anyone lurked in the shadows of the deck. Nothing.

Maybe he was too on edge from the day. It had exploded around him. What had started out to be a straightforward drive to chat with local law enforcement about the case and to meet with Aaliyah Terrence had him hearing things now. That was what happened when you were shot at, when dogs unburied old graves, and when a beautiful woman tried her hardest to hold back angry tears in the wake of the unsolved murder of her mother.

A shadow swept along the edge of his vision, and Wade twisted. A car drove by. He heard the echoing bark of a dog from several homes down the road. Another sweeping surveillance of Aaliyah's yard and the neighboring area left Wade reticent to relax. He had always had this thing about him. His gut. An instinct. And it told him that something was about to go dreadfully wrong. He would be there when it did.

The knock on her front door interrupted her conversation with her elderly neighbor, Charlie, who had brought over fresh banana bread that he'd baked that afternoon. They were already standing in the hallway just by the door, and the knock made her jump.

"Expectin' visitors?" The stoop-shouldered man lifted untrimmed gray eyebrows.

"Not really," Aaliyah answered. She couldn't help but be grateful that Charlie was there—though she wasn't sure how much protection the aged Vietnam War veteran would give her if the killer happened to be standing opposite her front door.

Then again, in spite of the unpredictable events of the day, it wasn't customary for a killer to knock politely.

Another rap on the door resulted in Charlie's, "Need me to get it?" He eyed her from under the brim of his well-worn, sweat-stained cowboy hat.

Aaliyah shook the remnants of fear from her mind. She

ignored the fact she still had the arrowhead bracelet from her truck stuffed in her jeans pocket. She'd picked it up with a tissue and then dropped it into a plastic storage baggie when she'd gotten home. Maybe there'd be evidence on it? Something to identify the killer? She should get it to Buck. But for now, she was distracted first by Charlie and then by whoever this was at her front door.

A *woof* by her side gave her courage, and Aaliyah reached down to draw comfort from Peaches as she opened the door.

"Oh. It's you." Her flat tone of voice in addressing Wade Marlowe must have emboldened Charlie's curiosity. He nudged alongside her, his shoulder brushing hers as he snuck a look at her visitor. His eyebrows rose.

"It's just Detective Marlowe," Aaliyah explained more thoroughly for her neighbor's sake.

"Just?" Charlie choked back a chuckle. He sniffed, giving no effort to hiding his old-man glee. "You got a young codger at your door, and you're just callin' him a 'just'?"

Aaliyah ignored Charlie and opened the door wider for Wade, who stood with an expression that could only be described as bemused. He stuck out his hand to shake Charlie's.

"Wade Marlowe," he stated.

"Charlie Beedle."

The handshake was one-hundred-percent male and not at all inclusive to Aaliyah. This was *her* house after all. She frowned as the two men sized one another up. There was a flicker in Wade's eyes she couldn't decipher. Charlie, on the other hand, chuckled without disguising it.

"Our girl here hasn't had a date since her boyfriend up and left her for that looker from out East. What he ever saw in her over this girl, I'll never know." Charlie clucked his tongue, not unlike a prying old woman. He waved his hand toward Aaliyah's kitchen. "I bring her food now and then, to make sure the girl eats." Charlie eyed Aaliyah. "And you best eat that up, 'cause tomorrow I'm baking some zucchini bread with the zucchinis from Mrs. Hanister's garden."

"Charlie, I—" Aaliyah wanted to correct his conclusion about Wade being her date as quickly as possible. "Detective Marlowe is—"

"Nope, nope." Charlie held his palm up, cutting off Aaliyah's words. He edged his way between her and Wade and out the front door. "No one's goin' to put blame on me for messin' up a good thing. You two have a grand ol' time." He wagged a stubby finger at Wade. "Have her home by midnight. I'll be watchin'. I live across the way over there in that green house."

Wade cleared his throat. "Yes, sir."

Aaliyah shot him a glare. He could have at least corrected Charlie. The dear man had good intentions but was as nosey as a hound in a prairie dog hole and twice as assertive.

Wade stepped inside, and Aaliyah closed the red door behind him. "Sorry about that," she muttered.

"No problem." Wade was at least decent enough to give Peaches some attention, she had to give him that. Peaches was completely disloyal to her misgivings toward the man and cozied up to Wade like he was her long-lost master. "She's a good dog," Wade acknowledged.

"The best." Aaliyah knew her response was clipped, but she hadn't recovered from the day, let alone the bombshell Wade Marlowe had dropped on her that afternoon. She had already planned to call Buck and tell him about the bracelet she'd found in her truck, but with Wade here, she knew she should say something now. But she didn't. She couldn't push her concerned words past her irritation.

"Can I help you with something?" She hadn't been home long when Charlie had arrived with the bread, so she still felt discombobulated. Aaliyah headed toward her small kitchen and Wade followed.

That was a tad assumptive of him. But, Aaliyah supposed, he was used to nosing around in other people's business. She plopped the banana bread on the counter and mustered her Montana politeness, drilled into her since childhood by her parents.

"Can I get you something to drink?"

Wade nodded. "I'd take a glass of water."

"Ice?" she offered, reaching for a glass from the open-faced cupboard.

"Sure."

Aaliyah took advantage of being able to stay busy digging for ice in the ice drawer of her freezer.

"I was hoping you would be willing to chat some more."

Aaliyah heard Wade ease himself onto a barstool that scooted up against the granite top bar in her kitchen. She took a few more seconds under the pretense of fumbling for ice to compose herself. Impulse made her want to rail at him. No, she didn't want to chat some more! After today? She really wanted that good cry she'd been aching for. Some Peaches snuggles. Not more time with the man who seemed intent on upending her life in twenty-four hours.

Regardless, Aaliyah turned to face him. "I get you have questions, but I'm not up to them tonight. I'm sorry." She wasn't really sorry, but maybe if she said so, Wade would simply leave as any good soul would do.

Whether he intended to manipulate her good conscience or not, Aaliyah noticed him wince a tad as he adjusted the

arm that had been grazed by the bullet. His brown eyes
were like cups of espresso mixed with sentimental angst
that tugged at her resolve.

"I get it," was all Wade said. But there was a sigh in his
voice. One that made Aaliyah draw in a resigned breath.

"Fine." She leaned back against the counter after setting the glass of water in front of him. "What do you want
to know?"

Wade turned the glass between his hands, the bottom
clinking along the granite and leaving moisture circles
smeared across the black polished stone. He seemed to
measure his words carefully as he met her eyes. "First, I
wanted to clear something up."

Uh-oh. Aaliyah crossed her arms over her chest in a protective hold, waiting for another bomb to drop.

Wade cleared his throat, and his gaze speared hers with
a sort of haunted hurt that shocked her. "I've not always
been on this side of the fence."

She frowned, confused.

He seemed to recognize her confusion and continued.
"You said this afternoon that I was always on this side of
murder. That I wasn't part of the victim's family, having
to process it all."

Aaliyah's heart squeezed with guilt. She had a feeling
she knew what he was going to say next even though it
was only her gut that gave her reason to assume anything.

He complied. "My sister—she was murdered a few years
ago. I know what it feels like to be the family—to hear those
words and know someone who means everything to you
has been stolen from you. Permanently. It's a major reason
why I do what I do." Wade lifted his glass and took a sip
of water before continuing. "I don't get any joy from this,

Aaliyah. But I do find that getting justice for the victim and their family makes it worthwhile."

"You want to help," Aaliyah concluded for him, blinking fast to avoid the tears that had been building all day. She spun so her back was to him and pretended to get her own glass of room temperature water from the faucet. "I get that you want to help. But you have to understand—I've not explored my birth history yet. I don't even know *what* to feel, and now? What you said, about Deborah Platt, about Lori what's-her-name claiming to be my aunt—"

"She *is* your aunt," Wade interrupted. "DNA—"

"DNA doesn't make them family." Aaliyah's words bit off whatever else Wade was going to say. She twisted back around to face off with him. "My parents adopted me. *They* are my family. I have Buck—my godfather—and even Gordon. I don't need to reconnect with biological extended family and kick a hornet's nest of trouble."

Wade's lips thinned, but he didn't say anything.

Aaliyah finished, leaned toward him, hoping he'd get the point. "If Deborah Platt is your cold case victim, and even if she's my biological mother, please leave me out of it. Especially after today. If there *are* ties from Deborah's old cold case to the graves Peaches discovered—I really want to stay as far away from it as possible."

But could she? That was a big looming question, and all it would take to dump her right back into the middle of it would be to pull out the arrowhead bracelet encased in its plastic bag from her pocket and show it to Wade. She had a feeling the entire day would break wide open again.

"I don't believe you're telling me everything." Wade's tone grew steely and stole any more words from Aaliyah's mouth.

She drew back in surprise. "Wha—I'm not *hiding* anything from you." Oops. She was. Her hand instinctively went into her pocket. It wasn't that she didn't *want* to report the bracelet, she just didn't want to report it to *him*.

Wade stiffened and his fingers tightened around his glass. He didn't drop his dark stare, and it captured Aaliyah's both with its intensity and its conviction. "You say your parents adopted you and your adoption records are court-ordered sealed."

"Yes." Aaliyah nodded, clipping her answer.

"How do you explain the backpack then? The fact that you were found behind the local church in the alley?"

Aaliyah stared at him, completely lost at his questions. "What are you talking about?"

Wade raised his eyebrows. "How do you have court-sealed adoption records as an abandoned baby? It would all be out there as a public record. Your story must have even made the local paper. There wouldn't be anything *sealed* about an abandoned newborn baby being discovered and taken in by a local couple."

If the counter hadn't been behind her, Aaliyah more than likely would have collapsed to the kitchen floor. As it was, she still had to brace herself by grabbing the door on the fridge for extra stability.

"My…parents told me my files are sealed. I've never seen them! I don't know what you're—what are you saying?"

Wade tilted his head as if he hadn't expected her response. "Buck told me your story this afternoon."

"What story?" Aaliyah's nausea twisted her stomach. Buck knew a *story* about her adoption? A pang of betrayal poked her heart.

Wade had the decency to don a sheepish expression. "I thought you knew. I thought you—" He composed himself, and everything about his expression told Aaliyah he was summoning the willpower to push through his hesitancy. "The sheriff—Buck—told me you were found as a baby, just a day or two old, behind the church. Your parents adopted you legally, yes, but not because they'd applied at an adoption agency."

Aaliyah's disbelief was coupled with dread. If what Wade Marlowe said was true—and what reason did he have to lie to her?—then that meant both Buck *and* her parents had been hiding these details since her birth. And what about everyone else in town? Had they all been keeping this secret from her? The realization shrouded her loyalty to her parents and to Buck in the first real question of doubt. Buck had acted so—so bewildered this afternoon when Wade had announced the DNA match between her and the old cold case victim, Deborah Platt. He hadn't known that detail—had he? No.

"Why would Buck tell you about my abandonment as a baby and not me?" She blurted out the first thing that came to mind, wildly swiping at a renegade tear that escaped her resolve.

Wade held up his hand, whether to inspire her not to react or to help calm her down, she didn't know. "I'm sorry, I thought you were aware of the circumstances around your adoption. Buck offered me the info this afternoon after you left the station."

"He just offered it up like an ice cream cone?" Aaliyah heard the watery incredulity in her own voice. The betrayal stung. It smarted with the same deep-rooted fear she'd always tried to hold at bay. That the ones closest to her were also the ones who could do her the most harm.

"I may have asked some direct questions, but, yes, Buck was forthcoming with his information. I—"

Buck was forthcoming to Wade Marlowe but not *her*?

"Get out." Aaliyah tried to disguise the panic rising in her with her own strong-willed command.

"Aaliyah, please, I didn't mean—"

"Get. Out." She hissed the words, but if she were truthful, her anger wasn't so much toward Wade as it was toward Buck. Toward his willing story told to a stranger when, apparently, Buck and her parents had kept it from her for twenty-five years.

Wade slid from the stool and gave her a polite nod. "My apologies."

Aaliyah stared at him.

He stared back, only his eyes were searching. If she read his expression right, he was trying to see if she was going to be all right as well as searching to see if she was being honest with him. Searching because Aaliyah knew Wade didn't completely trust her yet—or anyone at the moment.

After a day like today, could she blame him?

"One last question." He paused at the kitchen doorway, hand on the door frame. "Your neighbor friend, Charlie? Does he have a thing for arrowhead bracelets?"

Aaliyah frowned, disoriented by the sudden change in conversation.

"I saw he was wearing an arrowhead necklace—I was just curious—"

Understanding dawning, Aaliyah's voice was low and controlled when she interrupted. "Everyone in Montana owns something with an arrowhead on it. If you think for one minute that Charlie is behind the burial grounds—behind Deborah Platt's murder—" Aaliyah bit off her words.

She couldn't listen anymore. She couldn't *think* anymore. Today had exploded and the shrapnel was still flying hours later.

* * *

Well, that had gone well. Wade grimaced as he strode down the walk away from Aaliyah's house. This time, he wasn't scanning the yard for hiding places for a perpetrator, he was scanning himself for his lack of tact. It wasn't like him to bully his way into a conversation and lay out facts like he was proving a court case. Besides, sure he'd had questions about Aaliyah's adoption, how it related to Deborah Platt and her unsolved murder, and of course, he wanted to know how it all might relate to today's events! But mostly? He'd come here to try to smooth things over with the red-headed forest ranger, and instead, he'd made her cry. Again.

Wade wrenched open his car door, irritated at himself. He'd learned long ago that it was wise to start conversations with prayer. Maybe not out loud and formal, but at least ask God for the words before beginning. Had he even done that tonight? Or were his own wounds because of Amy's murder still so raw that it distorted his thinking?

Wade slid into the front seat and patted for his car key in the side pocket of his jacket. He let out a frustrated growl and bent his head. He'd left his jacket in Aaliyah's house. He needed his car key—he needed his hotel key card too—and they were both in the jacket he'd tossed over the back of the barstool in Aaliyah's kitchen.

Wade exited the car. She would be so happy to see him again! With that wry internalization, Wade made his way through the night's darkness and back up the walk to Aaliyah's red front door.

"I'm sorry. I left my jacket. I'll just be a minute," Wade rehearsed in his mind.

A scream and a crash jolted him from his distracted thoughts. Wade froze, his body on instant alert. His left hand felt for the gun holstered at his waist. The sidearm felt familiar in his hands as he hurried toward the house.

Another scream and Wade wasted no time. Thankful the front door was still unlocked, he shoved it open, shouting his entry as he did so.

"Police!"

Aaliyah's scream came from a room to the left of the kitchen. Unfamiliar with the house, Wade moved fast but with caution, his gun held in front of him.

The sound of glass breaking sent Wade into the next room, a small dining area. He swept the room, but it was empty. As he turned to clear the hallway just off to his right, something solid came from behind and struck between his shoulder blades.

Wade grunted as his assailant's attack shoved him into the dining table. He struggled to maintain a grip on his firearm, twisting as he did so, raising it in defense.

The attacker loomed over Wade in the fast-fading remaining light of dusk that filtered in the windows. A baseball bat swung and connected with Wade's wrist. The pain of his already wounded arm and the impact of the bat sent Wade's gun flying across the room. The bat rose again, but this time, Wade rolled off the table to the floor as the bat swung downward and smashed onto the polished wooden tabletop.

Wade reached for the attacker's ankle and yanked.

With a grunt, the man stumbled and careened to the floor. The ski mask on his face was pulled partially off to reveal the side of a jaw and chin, but nothing else.

They wrestled, both fighting for the hold that would give them the upper hand. Wade leveled a strong blow into the man's rib cage, but the man was undeterred. He wrapped his arms around Wade's middle, yanking him to his feet and shoving him hard. The motion caused Wade to lose his footing, and he careened backward, his shoulders crashing into a corner curio cabinet. Glass shattered around him as his body smashed against the shelves. Wade's head connected with the side frame of the cabinet, dazing his senses. He held up his arms in a defensive motion to avoid the next blow, but the sound of vicious barking broke into the room.

A guttural shout and a curse released from the assailant, and he sprinted from the room, Aaliyah's Lab fast on his heels. Wade moaned, holding his head between his palms, attempting to regain his senses. He wanted to chase after the invader, but with the room spinning, the first few steps he took were wobbly and disoriented.

Peaches padded back into the room, panting, her tongue lolling from the side of her mouth. She sniffed at Wade, pressing her muzzle against his leg. He reached down.

"I'm okay. Good girl, Peaches." Scratching the dog's ear, Wade blinked repeatedly, willing the room to cease its infernal spinning. "Where's your momma, huh? Go find Aaliyah."

The dog seemed to comprehend, and she bounded from the room, her brown eyes bright with doggy pride at defending her mistress and home. Wade followed, each step bringing back more of his equilibrium.

"Aaliyah?" he called out and was greeted by a weak "In here." He stepped through a doorway into a bedroom. Aaliyah was pulling herself from the floor, grasping the bed for support. A trail of blood dripped down the side of her face. "Are you okay?" Wade hurried to help her rise, and for a second, they both stood facing one another, hands gripping the other's forearms for support. Peaches pranced between them as though she expected a treat for her bravery—which was definitely going on Wade's list of things to do.

But first, Aaliyah.

He tilted his head to better assess her injury. Pushing some of her hair from her face, he gauged the cut at her temple. It wasn't as bad as it appeared. Head wounds bled like nobody's business, and he was relieved to see it wasn't an emergency-type injury.

"I need to call backup." Wade fished in his pocket for his phone.

"I already called Buck." Aaliyah sank onto the bed. "Actually, I called 911 first."

Sirens in the distance confirmed Aaliyah's statement. Wade watched as Peaches pushed her way between Aaliyah's knees and nosed her hands. A small whine captured Aaliyah's attention, and she turned to meet her dog's need for reassurance. She bent over Peaches, planting a kiss on the dog's head. "I'm fine, baby girl," she crooned, then she looked up at Wade. A pained honesty reflected in her eyes. "Thank you for…coming to rescue me."

They'd gotten off to a rocky start, and it had been one day filled with enough action to last a lifetime as far as Wade was concerned.

"Did you get a look at the attacker at all?" Wade got down to business, standing over Aaliyah as she clung to her dog for comfort.

She shook her head. "Not with that ski mask on."

"What happened?"

"I don't know." Aaliyah shook her head. "You left and I came back here to change, and the window was open." She pointed to it. It overlooked one of the sketchy areas of the yard that Wade had noticed earlier would be a good place for someone to hide. "Then he came out of nowhere."

The sirens were gaining in volume now, and Wade prepared to head to the front door to greet them. But he paused in the doorway. "Did he say anything when he attacked you?"

"No." Aaliyah's voice caught with emotion, but Wade chose to ignore it to save her pride as she swiped quickly at her tears. She finished, lifting watery eyes to his. "He just attacked. I think—I think he meant to kill me."

Wade's gut clenched at the way Aaliyah stared up at him with both disbelief and question. The assailant's appearance only confirmed his earlier theory that he must think Aaliyah could identify him. Why else would they have risked such exposure twice more in the same day? There was a desperation to the action, and a compulsion to be rid of Aaliyah that left Wade not only concerned but also extremely suspicious.

If the killer thought she could identify him, then he would get more desperate. If the killer knew Aaliyah hadn't seen him clearly enough—and the fact he'd worn a ski mask made Wade believe that the killer held some doubts—then what was the additional motivation to act so aggressively in a way that put the killer right in the center of the investigation? His appearance at the secluded graveyard was one thing and could potentially be explained away by the fact the killer must have returned to retrieve his arrowhead bracelet—the one Aaliyah had found. But later? With the area teeming with investigators and the authorities? The killer had risked being caught when he'd chased down Aaliyah and when he'd grazed Wade with a bullet. Now this? Tonight? In Aaliyah's own home?

"Do you think this is personal?" Wade ventured aloud.

Aaliyah stared at him. "Why? Do *you*?" she countered.

Wade's eyes caught a glimpse of something on the floor by her feet. He bent to retrieve it. The black woven thread of a bracelet with an arrowhead charm was encased in a plastic baggie. His hand closed around it as if by capturing the killer's calling card, he could capture the killer.

His eyes met Aaliyah's, and he answered her question with conviction in his voice. "Yeah. Yeah, I do think it's personal."

FOUR

Aaliyah saw Wade scoop up the bracelet. It must have fallen from her jeans pocket in the scuffle. She had *thought* she'd prefer to confide in Buck about that, but the reminder of his prior dishonesty struck her again. Maybe Wade would be safer. Maybe he could be trusted and Buck couldn't.

The first responders entered her house, and the next several minutes were a blur. After a butterfly bandage was applied to the cut on her temple, the EMTs advised her to allow them to transport her to the hospital for a full examination. She'd been hit on the head that morning, and now tonight. Aaliyah pushed away their concerns.

"I just want to stay home," she argued. "I'm fine. I bumped my head on the windowsill when I got knocked down. That's all."

"Aaliyah—" Wade interrupted.

"No." Aaliyah held her hand up and retorted more sharply than she'd intended. She tried to soften her voice. "I'm sorry, I just want today to be over."

The EMT spoke in a low tone to Wade. Aaliyah could tell neither of them were happy with her refusal of further treatment.

A few police officers roamed the house and the grounds. Red and blue lights from squad cars lit up the neighborhood. Heavy footsteps on the walk outside alerted Aaliyah to the entrance of another newcomer to the scene.

Buck charged into the room, the ferocity on his face like that of a raging bull. "What happened!" It was a demand for information, not a question, and it was aimed at Wade, not her. The older man wrapped Aaliyah in his strong arms, but she stiffened. She ached to drink in the comfort of the sheriff's familiarity. All of her life, he'd been as much of a steadfast foundation for her as her own adoptive parents. But now? In a split moment of revelation, things had changed.

"I'm all right." Aaliyah pushed away from Buck. His brows furrowed, but he didn't ask questions. Aaliyah continued before Wade took the lead. It was her house; it was her life. While she appreciated him being there and coming to the rescue, she didn't need the outsider detective to speak for her. "Someone was in the house after Wade left. I don't know if they'd broken in before I arrived home, or how they were there. But I'm all right."

"But it was a direct attack on Aaliyah," Wade interjected.

Buck issued her a stern look. "You're going to the hospital."

"No. I'm not." Aaliyah bit back her anxiety and frustration. While she appreciated the strong protective natures of these men, she also needed her space. Especially from Buck. Hopefully not forever, but at least for tonight.

Another voice broke into the group.

"I said have her home by midnight, not cause a ruckus!" It was Charlie, and his bent frame ambled into the room with a relaxed air that made Aaliyah finally feel like smiling.

Charlie sidled up to Wade and eyed him. "You look like you took a bit of a beating."

For the first time, Aaliyah took notice of Wade's own injuries. She'd been so consumed by the shock of the evening that she'd not paid attention to Wade's darkening black eye, the split at his lip and the way he hugged his arm around his midsection.

"Are *you* okay?" she asked, knowing full well how belated it was.

Wade shrugged off the concern. "I'm fine."

No one questioned his dismissal of the need for medical care. How come a man could brush it off and people listened, but she couldn't refuse it without a barrage of arguments?

The next several moments were filled with questions from Buck and the investigating officer. Wade showed Buck the arrowhead bracelet, and Aaliyah didn't miss the look the men exchanged between them.

"What is it?" She inserted herself between them, determining to tell Buck later that the bracelet had fallen from her pocket. She'd also tell him where she'd found it. All of it was pertinent and probably critical information, but for some reason, she felt the need to keep Wade Marlowe at arm's length. He'd disrupted her life in the last twenty-four hours with the chaos of a hurricane. She needed separation from him. "What aren't you both saying?" she insisted but directed her question to Buck.

Buck's chest heaved with a heavy sigh of resignation. He waved a hand at Wade. "Tell her, Marlowe."

Wade turned to Aaliyah, who waited, unwilling to look away from the detective's dark eyes even though they did things to her stomach that could—on a better day—be compared to melted, molten chocolate.

"Your mother's cold case—" he began.

"She's not my mother. She's my *birth* mother," Aaliyah corrected.

"Sorry." Wade gave a short nod of apology. "Deborah Platt's case—when her remains were found, she was wearing an arrowhead bracelet."

Aaliyah let that sink in as Wade continued.

"There's a really good chance today's discovery of the graves, plus your witness of the arrowhead bracelet at the gravesites, and now this bracelet," Wade lifted the bagged bracelet for her to see as if she'd not seen it before, "are all connected to Deborah's case."

"The same killer?" Charlie interrupted.

Both Buck and Wade shot the elderly man a look. Aaliyah bit back an amused smile. It appeared they'd forgotten the man was there too. She noticed Wade's gaze drop to the arrowhead necklace around Charlie's wrinkled neck.

"Do you remember anything from back in the day when the unidentified remains were discovered?" Wade countered Charlie's question with his own.

Buck cleared his throat and shifted nervously. He reached out and tapped Charlie's arm. "Best you get on home, don't you think, Charlie?"

Aaliyah didn't miss Wade's quick glance at Buck, nor the way his brows furrowed in confusion.

Charlie sniffed and nodded. He made fast work of his goodbyes, and for a brief moment, Aaliyah considered how quickly the older man moved for the front door. Far more quickly than she'd seen him amble in the past.

Wade leaned in toward Buck, irritation in his voice. "What was that about?" he demanded.

Buck gave his head a quick shake. "Charlie Beedle wouldn't hurt a fly. I know what you were thinking, boy."

Wade's eyes darkened at the subtle patronization.

Aaliyah readjusted her position by the two men, uncomfortable with the tension that was filling the air.

"We need to let Aaliyah get some rest." Buck didn't even try to disguise his evasiveness.

Aaliyah nodded, thankful the authorities were already clearing out. Nothing new had been found. The house had been fully swept, windows checked and secured, and door locks verified to be in full working order.

"I'll stay." Wade's declaration startled Aaliyah.

"No, you won't," she declared. He had a lot of nerve just inserting himself into her business. It might be related to his cold case, but he had no jurisdiction over her life. "I'll be fine." There was no way Aaliyah would admit the idea of being here alone for the rest of the night frightened her. But if things got too freaky, she could drive to her parents'. They lived outside of Park Springs on their small ranch, and she was sure by morning, once they'd heard about all the events, they'd be insisting she come there anyway.

"Please." Aaliyah opted for a gentler approach. She eyed Wade cautiously but tried to infuse a bit of warmth into her voice. "I'll be fine. Really, I will."

His look told her he didn't believe her for one minute.

"Whoever broke in and attacked me wouldn't try it again tonight. Not after all of this." She swept her hand toward the squad cars still bathing the neighborhood in red and blue lights.

"He's already tried three times today to get rid of you." Wade wasn't going to be easy to convince.

"And three strikes, he's out." Aaliyah's quip made Buck smile, but then he grew serious.

"Wade is right, Aaliyah. You should consider someone staying with you or let me drive you out to your folks' place."

Aaliyah shook her head. "I have Peaches. I need to be home, Buck. Please."

Both men eyed her with regretful acquiescence.

She had won, but Aaliyah hoped she was right. Somehow, she couldn't help but wonder if the killer was watching, even now, and waiting for his next opportunity to strike.

Wade wasn't sure if he should smile or grimace at Aaliyah's response to his text the next morning. On waking in his hotel room, he'd rolled over and shot a message off to her.

All good? Checking in to make sure you're safe.

He'd watched as the text was immediately marked as Read, and then the chat bubble popped up. It stayed up for some time and then disappeared. Finally, after what seemed like an eternity, his phone pinged with her response.

Yep.

Yep? Wade had mused on the one-word answer through his shower and his continental breakfast in the hotel lounge, and he still mused on it as he sat at the desk back in his room, reviewing the Deborah Platt cold case files for the hundredth time.

There it was.

He knew something had been off last night at Aaliyah's between Buck and Charlie Beedle. This was it. Wade reread the information that listed Charlie Beedle as a person of interest back in the original investigation. At that time, with Deborah Platt's remains being unidentified, there hadn't been much to go on. Even DNA had its limitations back then.

Why had Charlie been questioned?

The same reason Wade had been cautiously suspicious of the pleasant elderly man last night.

Deborah Platt's body had been found with an arrowhead bracelet. Charlie Beedle had, at that time, owned a small tourist gift shop that specialized in arrowhead jewelry.

Too coincidental? Maybe. But as Wade hiked up the walk to Charlie's front door, he admitted it deserved being revisited. He paused on the step, turning to assess Aaliyah's house across the way. A light was on in the main room. All seemed peaceful. Whether she liked it or not, he'd check in with her once he was finished chatting with Charlie.

The door opened before Wade could knock.

Charlie's bushy eyebrows were raised and wrinkled along with his forehead. His peppery gray hair was mussed, and he held a coffee mug in his hand as though he was prepared for a chat.

"Figured you'd show up." Charlie stepped aside, and Wade entered the house.

Charlie Beedle might be aged, but he hadn't lost any of his mental faculties. There was a sharp awareness in his eyes that put Wade on alert.

The smell of cinnamon permeated the air, and Wade's stomach growled, much to his annoyance.

Charlie smirked. "Zucchini bread's in the oven. I told Aaliyah I'd bring her some later this morning." He held out his hand to a circular wooden dining table with four chairs positioned around it. "Have a seat. Want some coffee?"

"No, I'm good," Wade responded.

Charlie eased onto a chair opposite of the one Wade

claimed. His arthritic hands cupped his coffee mug. "Here to ask me about the old cold case, aren't you?"

"Yes, sir." Wade nodded. He leaned forward, resting his elbows on the table. "You were questioned as a person of interest back in the day."

"I was." Charlie's confirmation was accompanied by an unblinking, direct stare. "They found nothing on me too. I had nothing to do with it."

"Tell me about your arrowhead jewelry." Wade pointed to the necklace around Charlie's neck.

"What's to tell?" Charlie took a noisy sip of his coffee. "I'm a crafty codger. I bake, I make jewelry. I can even crochet an afghan if you need one."

"Did you recognize the bracelet that was found with the victim?"

"Twenty-five years ago? Sure." Charlie's nod gave Wade pause. "It was the same cheap jewelry you find in half the tourist shops across the US of A. Nothing unusual about it at all. The killer left a calling card, or else the gal that was killed was wearing it 'cause it was hers. To my knowledge, they never figured that out."

"It wasn't one of your bracelets?" Wade pressed.

Charlie's eyes narrowed. "I told you, it was cheap jewelry. I make good jewelry. Quality stuff."

Which was exactly why Wade was questioning Charlie. If the bracelet Aaliyah had seen yesterday at the gravesites was any clue, it stated that the killer appreciated well-crafted arrowhead jewelry when it came to himself. He'd returned for the bracelet. He'd almost killed Aaliyah over it. He glanced at Charlie's wrist. There was no bracelet. But then, the killer wouldn't be that foolish as to parade it on his wrist after yesterday's events. Would he?

Charlie cleared his throat and eyed Wade with a stark

gaze. "I'll tell you this, Detective. I fought in Vietnam. I sucked in enough Agent Orange to earn me benefits from the government and get me admitted ten years ago to the hospital with cancer. I may have beat that, but I'm in no way in any shape to be traipsing through the Bob, burying bodies, dropping arrowhead bracelets made in China with the victims and then coming back to town and launching an assault on my neighbor."

Well, Charlie knew exactly what Wade had been considering, and now he'd called him out on it. Wade wasn't deterred. He worked his jaw back and forth and then drew in a deep breath. "I thank you for your time, then." There wasn't anything more to say or do at this point. Wade had to admit, even as Charlie walked him to the door, that the man would have had to be far more fit to be capable of yesterday's events. But then, with how direct Charlie was, Wade wasn't convinced that he wasn't a good actor as well.

Charlie gave him a small wave as Wade took his leave. "Hope you figure out who killed that gal back in the day, and what's goin' on with those graves in the Bob."

"Me too," Wade responded.

Charlie's parting words bounced off Wade's back as he jogged toward Aaliyah's place. "I'll be bringing that zucchini bread over around eleven!"

Wade halted, confused, until he saw that Charlie was shouting over him to Aaliyah, who stood on her porch staring at them both.

As Charlie returned inside his home, Aaliyah started toward Wade with Peaches padding along behind her. She met him at the end of her drive. Her hazel eyes sparked with something Wade couldn't quite interpret, and her very kissable mouth was pursed as if she were either irritated or confused. Kissable mouth? He shoved that thought aside as far as he could push it. Now was not the time to be attracted to a woman who'd almost gotten him—not to mention herself—killed yesterday.

"Were you interrogating Charlie?" Aaliyah's eyes snapped.

Yep. Definitely irritation.

"No. I was asking him some questions."

"About?" Aaliyah crossed her arms over her yellow T-shirt. She must have taken the day off. Her complexion appeared even brighter and softer now that she wasn't in forest ranger khaki.

"Did you know he was a suspect in the Deborah Platt case?" Wade bit his tongue. He probably shouldn't have said that, but she had a way of getting him off his guard, and he wasn't quite sure how to handle that.

"That's ridiculous." Aaliyah tilted her head. "And you think he's behind all of yesterday too, huh?"

"No." Wade's answer seemed to take her aback. Aaliyah's defensive posture softened. "I don't think he's capable of it—at least, not acting alone. And there's no evidence to suggest we've got more than one killer on our hands. But I'd still like to know if he has anything to offer that could help with the case."

"That's fair." Aaliyah glanced at the watch on her wrist. "I need to get going. My parents heard about yesterday, and I need to head to their place and calm them down."

Wade appreciated that though she didn't owe him an explanation, she was still offering it.

She moved to pass him and head to her truck with the dog, but he reached out and stopped her with a light touch to her arm. Her soft skin against his fingertips stilled him for a moment.

Aaliyah lifted her eyes.

"Stay alert, okay?" he prompted.

She nodded and hurried away.

Wade breathed a quick prayer as her truck revved into life. God was going to have to do some serious protecting today. Not just from the Arrowhead Killer—which Wade was beginning to think of him as—but also from his own heart, which was getting way too involved with Aaliyah Terrence's welfare, and far too quickly.

Aaliyah glanced at Peaches, who sat sentinel in the passenger seat of her truck. She'd just spent the last few hours with her parents, and now she couldn't stop shaking. Her fingers gripped the steering wheel until her knuckles were white.

They had lied to her. All of her life, they had lied to her!

She had confronted them with the information that Wade had given her last night—the story about being abandoned behind the church and the subsequent adoption. It all sounded so ridiculous, but the moment she'd laid it out in question form for her parents and she'd seen the look on her mom's face, Aaliyah knew that Wade Marlowe had his facts right.

Not just Buck, but her parents, had deceived her. What else hadn't they told her? How had something like her birth, abandonment and adoption not made the local papers at the time? Park Springs wasn't a big town. It felt like everyone knew everyone here. But her parents had told her they'd kept the discovery of her super confidential. For her safety. There'd never even been a newspaper article about her as an abandoned baby.

Wade Marlowe had been the interloper yesterday, and now? Now Aaliyah was tempted to believe he was the only person she could trust.

She'd even called Buck on the way to her parents' to tell him about the arrowhead bracelet left in her truck yesterday. He'd been none too happy that she'd not alerted him to it immediately, not to mention allowed him and Wade to believe it had been left at the scene of the attack last night.

Aaliyah stifled a deep sigh as she turned toward the local feed store. She needed to pick up food for Peaches, and then she really should check in with Gordon, her partner at the ranger station. She was certain the area where she'd uncovered the burial grounds of the killer was still being scoured, and that meant Gordon probably had his hands full with questions from not only the authorities, but also local ranchers and out-of-state campers who were roughing it in the wilderness.

"But first, food for you, Peaches." Aaliyah spoke aloud and the dog turned her head, tongue hanging and her jowls pulled up in a dog smile. Aaliyah allowed herself a small laugh, hoping to break the tension and anxiety that was roiling in her gut.

The feed store was up ahead, its building on the outskirts of town and set apart from other franchises and shops. Aaliyah turned her truck into the parking lot just as her phone pinged. Wade's number flashed on the screen, but she tapped her phone to ignore it, wrenching it from its holder on the dash and stuffing it into the pocket of her leggings. Her phone pinged again, and she thought better of it and slipped it back out of her pocket, answering Wade's call.

"Hello?" She leaned against her truck in the mostly empty parking lot.

"Just checking in," Wade stated.

"You're worse than my mom." Aaliyah afforded him a laugh, and then her stomach clenched with the memory of the conversation she'd just had with her parents.

"Can't be too careful." Wade's voice had a husky quality to it that entranced her at the same time it made her cautious.

"Did you need something?" she inquired, eyeing the feed store and rolling the windows down just enough so Peaches would have some air while she went inside.

Wade's low, smooth chuckle raised goose bumps on her arms. Another time and another place and she'd probably start swooning like an actress in an old John Wayne Western. "I'm going to stop and grab some lunch at the diner before I head back to the station. Want to meet me there?"

Aaliyah held the phone away from her ear for a second and eyed it before returning it so she could answer. "Is this a date?"

Wade made a choking sound on the other end. She could tell he hadn't been expecting her candor. He cleared his throat. "Let's just say it's a get-off-on-the-right-foot kind of meeting. I think yesterday needs a redo, and I sort of owe you."

Yes, he did owe her. The upheaval his arrival in town had brought was second only to the fact she'd been confronted by a serial killer.

"Fine. I'll meet you there," she answered.

"Good. And, Aaliyah?" Wade's tone shifted to more serious.

"Yes?"

"Please be careful. After yesterday, you really shouldn't be out and about on your own."

"I have Peaches." She tossed a quick glance at her dog, who had laid her head between her paws and sprawled across the bench seat of the truck.

"She did a good job last night, but Labs aren't known for their ferocity," Wade retorted.

"I'll be fine." Aaliyah ended the call before he could respond again. She was already regretting telling him she'd meet him for lunch. It wasn't a good idea.

Aaliyah took the next several minutes to head into the feed store and heft a forty-pound bag of dog food onto a cart. The store wasn't typically swarming with customers, and today, she appreciated the fact she could do her pickup without having to make small talk with folks she knew. A teenager sat at the front counter and scanned the feed bag, paying more attention to his phone and oblivious to conversation that was typical with good customer service. Aaliyah paid for the dog food and then wheeled the cart to her pickup.

The golden hills beyond the lot rose to meet the blue sky dotted with fluffy white clouds. Days like today were the kind where she wanted to be working. To be out in the Bob, checking on campers, filing a report on a steer that'd been killed by a wolf pack, logging water levels on the south fork of the Flathead River and spending way too much time daydreaming beneath the expansive Montana sky. Instead, she was taking a day off because Gordon thought she should. Sometimes, what people didn't understand was that it was better to face trauma head on than try to rest and recover. Besides, today was giving her far too much think time.

Aaliyah slammed the tailgate of her truck into place after hefting the bag of dog food into the bed. She really needed to—

Her thought was cut short as an arm snaked around her throat from behind. She was tugged backward, all ability to scream cut off by the suffocating strength of the arm squeezing against her neck and her jawline. Spots danced in front of her eyes. She clawed at the arm, sheathed in a cotton shirt, her fingernails digging into the skin beneath.

Aaliyah flailed, pushing backward against her assailant in an effort to lessen the pressure. Black shields closed in on the corners of her eyes as oxygen was cut off. He was strong—so strong! Fighting with everything in her, Aaliyah attempted to sink to the ground, allowing her legs to buckle at the knees in hopes the sudden sag of her body would surprise her attacker. But it didn't. He moved with her, hauling her up by the stranglehold in the isolated parking lot.

A distant bark from Peaches in the cab of her truck met Aaliyah's ears. She kicked with her feet, connecting with the man's shin in an insufficient last attempt to free herself. The blue sky turned black as Aaliyah warred to keep conscious.

"Just give in." The words were hot in her ear, but unrecognizable as the man seemed to have a mask over his face muffling his voice. She felt the man's breath against her skin, the heave of the muscle in his arm, and then for a moment, he adjusted his grip on her, and she caught a flash of an arrowhead bracelet, gold linked chain, around a wrist.

The world went dark.

FIVE

Aaliyah moaned, rolling onto her side, the cement floor beneath her cool against her skin. Disoriented, she opened her eyes and was met with darkness. The killer. It had to be him. He'd abducted her from the feed store parking lot. As the memory returned to her, panic grew in the pit of her stomach. Where was she? Why hadn't he already killed her? Not that she wanted to be dead, but the fact she was bound with her wrists behind her back and her feet zip-tied at the ankles told her he had either had a stroke of conscience, or he still needed her for some reason she could not fathom.

At least she was alive. For now. And if Peaches was still in her truck at the feed lot, then hopefully someone would see her and notify Buck. Everyone in Park Springs knew her pickup truck, and everyone in Park Springs loved Peaches.

Aaliyah pushed off the floor as best as she could, using her core muscles to try to position herself on her backside. Once she'd managed to sit up, she tried to scan where she was being held. God knew where she was, and there was comfort in that.

"Please, please, please," she prayed aloud. Her voice was a throaty whisper.

Aaliyah could feel the bulge of her phone in her leggings pocket. Whoever had tied her up and put her here either hadn't been concerned that she'd be able to get to her phone or had been oblivious to the fact that she had it. The idea of connection gave her a surge of hope. If she could get her wrists free, she could try to call Buck—or Wade even—and get help.

Shadows opposite the wall from where Aaliyah sat seemed to be outlines of boxes. If she could scoot over to them, maybe there would also be something sturdier stacked there—perhaps with rough edges—that she could use as an abrasive edge to try to free herself from the plastic ties. Where she sat now, she had only a wall behind her, ridged metal and smooth beneath her touch.

Aaliyah used her feet and knees to push herself across the floor on her backside. She'd never considered how much balance it required to stay in a seated position when hands were bound and ankles tied together. Her breaths came in short, anxious gasps, and tears of worry burned her eyes, but she refused to give in.

"Come on, Terrence, you can do this," she coached herself. The sound of her own voice brought her courage, but then she bit down on her tongue. If her abductor was nearby—if he heard her—it could be the end of her.

Aaliyah felt grit against her skin. Sand and small stones. Her feet connected with a *thud* against the cardboard boxes. She twisted herself around on her backside, so she could feel where she was with her hands.

Cardboard was useless against zip ties. If she braced herself against the boxes, she could push herself into a standing position—however precarious—and maybe find something higher up that she could use to free herself.

After a few moments of unskilled gymnastics, Aaliyah shoved against the boxes until she could stand. Her fingers felt along the boxes, and she hopped to the side, feeling the next pile. A tarp met her fingertips, beneath it the hard feel of tall, narrow objects leaning against the wall. Hopeful, Aaliyah managed to push the tarp away enough to feel the hidden objects. Rough metal met her hands, and to her excitement, she felt the form of steel fence T-posts. They were worn and weathered. She could tell because the coating was chipped beneath her fingers, leaving a residue that felt like rust, and they had chiseled edges from years of use.

It was at least something.

Aaliyah positioned herself against them, her hands behind her back and her wrists crossed and held secure by the plastic ties. She felt along the edge of one post until she found the roughest point. It was by no means sharp, but it was, she hoped, abrasive enough that she could work the zip tie against it and weaken its hold.

"Please," she breathed again. If the last day and a half had taught her anything, it was that everything she'd ever known was founded on half-truths and secrets, and that safety was neither guaranteed nor owed. But one thing she had been taught from childhood was that God would never leave her or forsake her. Aaliyah hoped that was one truth that still stood strong—because all the others in her life seemed to be crashing down around her. "Please. Help me break these ties." Her whispered prayer accompanied the first swipe of her ties against the metal post.

She had to hurry. She had no idea when her abductor would return, but she had a strong suspicion it wasn't his intent to ever set her free.

He was being irrational, and Wade didn't appreciate that side of himself. It'd been over an hour that he'd sat waiting for Aaliyah at the round café table outside of the diner.

She hadn't arrived yet. A nervous anticipation was building in him.

Wade pulled out his phone and eyed it. No calls. No texts. Either she was standing him up—which was very possible—or something had happened. Maybe it wasn't irrational, considering the events of the last thirty-some hours, to be concerned. But it was irrational to just sit here and do nothing. Besides, he was here to solve Deborah Platt's cold case, and if that merged with the Arrowhead Killer and this new discovery of burial grounds, then sitting here was accomplishing absolutely nothing.

This was ridiculous. He'd just call her again, and if she thought he was suffocating in his protectiveness, fine. Wade lifted his phone to dial, but Buck's gruff voice interrupted him.

"Wade!" As he approached, the badge on his shirt caught a ray of sunshine and reflected it. Buck extended his hand, and Wade gave it a quick shake.

"Any updates?" Wade asked, glancing at the man accompanying Buck. He was dressed in forest ranger garb, his flat hat covering the same peppery gray hair as Buck's.

Buck gave a defeated shake of his head. "Nothing. No one saw anyone fleeing from Aaliyah's place last night." He turned to introduce the man beside him. "This is my brother, Gordon Halstead. He works with Aaliyah at the ranger station."

His interest piqued, Wade shook hands with the man, appreciating the eye contact and the firm grasp.

"Yesterday was quite the day in the Bob." Gordon's assessment was an understatement, which his facial expression seemed to acknowledge. "Man, I'm glad Aaliyah was all right."

"Me too," Wade acknowledged. "You're the one she called for help?"

"Yeah." Gordon winced. "We run into some things out there—grizzlies, lions, *campers* from out of state." They all chuckled with the mutual understanding of tourist campers who underestimated the Montana wilderness. "But I *never* expected her to find human remains."

"Gordon confirmed he's scoped that area out before and never seen the ground disturbed or anything suspicious," Buck added. "They've removed the remains from four graves. Each one had an arrowhead bracelet in it."

Wade exchanged a glance with Gordon, his eyes dropping to the man's wrists out of pure instinct, as he responded to Buck. "So, just like the one Deborah Platt was wearing when she was found two decades ago." Gordon's wrists were free of jewelry. In fact, the man was free of anything that didn't scream *Ranger*.

"Unfortunately, yes. We're looking at a serial killer." Buck nodded his head. "I'm glad we've got other departments working on this case. It's going to bust wide open soon."

Wade grimaced. Buck was right. Once the media got involved, the entire nation would turn their eyes to the Bob Marshall Wilderness and the Arrowhead Killer. Which meant maybe people would come further out of the woodwork about Deborah Platt's murder too. He directed his attention to Gordon. "Does the ranger who discovered Deborah Platt's remains still live in the area—do you know? I'd like to chat with him."

Gordon rubbed his chin, and his face twisted in consternation. "No, actually. He passed away about eight years ago. Never did talk about it either. I mean, I can't blame him." Gordon's chest heaved in an understanding sigh. "It's one thing to discover graves, an entirely other thing to discover a body that never made it to a grave."

Wade had read the crime scene report so much he practically had it memorized. Aaliyah's birth mother, Deborah Platt, had been found unburied, her body in extensive decomposition.

Aaliyah.

Wade pulled his phone from his jeans pocket and checked it again. Nothing. "Have either of you heard from Aaliyah in the past hour or so? She was going to meet up with me here, and I'm getting worried."

Buck's eyes narrowed with concern. "No. I talked to her earlier about the arrowhead bracelet she found in her truck yesterday, and I—"

"What?" Wade's sharp interruption cut off Buck's words.

"She didn't tell you?" Buck frowned.

"No." Wade snapped.

"The bracelet you found last night after her attack? It was actually one that fell from her pocket. It'd been left on the seat of her truck earlier in the afternoon. That's why it was in a baggie. Aaliyah had the forethought to bag it to preserve any evidence."

Air hissed between Gordon's teeth at his quick intake of breath. He eyed his brother Buck. "She's got a target on her back."

Wade nodded. "I'm going to call her."

The other two men waited for Wade as he dialed. A second went by and then static and the recorded voice of the cell carrier.

"The caller you are trying to reach is unavailable…"

Wade ended the call and eyed Buck and Gordon. "Her phone is either off or out of signal range. I'm not sitting around. I'm going to go find her."

Buck's hand shot out to stop Wade. His eyes were filled with concern. "Let's not get ahead of ourselves."

"She hasn't checked in, Sheriff." Wade opted for the man's more formal title. "Is that like Aaliyah to commit to being somewhere and not showing?" It was an honest question.

Gordon answered for the sheriff. "No. Aaliyah is extremely punctual and communicates better than almost anyone I know."

Wade eyed Buck with an element of sternness. He didn't want to step on the man's toes, but Buck's lack of urgency irked him. "Sheriff?"

Buck gave a quick nod. "Yeah. Yes. Let's see if we can track her down."

Wade fell into stride between Buck and Gordon. Of the three of them, all had a sense of protective responsibility over Aaliyah, but Wade was aware he was the one who knew her the least.

It seemed strange, then, that Buck—her mentor and a law enforcement lead—would have any hesitations at all.

Aaliyah's hands snapped apart, the zip tie breaking after what felt like hours of working it against the fence post. She brought her hands around to the front of her, hugging her wrists to her chest. They were sore and bruised, and she could feel them tingling from the lack of circulation. Without attempting to free her feet, she slid to the floor, reaching into her leggings pocket for her phone.

The screen lit at her touch, illuminating the room she was in. Most definitely a storage space, with boxes sealed and stacked to the ceiling, a wooden bed frame leaning against a wall, and now that she could see with her flashlight, a barrel at the far end housing garden rakes, shovels and a set of pruning shears hanging on the edge. She crawled toward them, reaching up to retrieve them while setting her phone flashlight up on the floor. One quick snip and her feet were free of their bindings. Leaping to her feet, Aaliyah checked for a signal. It was low, but she hit the call button, redialing the last number she'd spoken to. Wade.

The static on the other end was atrocious. She heard the phone ring once, then it dissipated into more static and then dead air.

"No, no, no," she muttered, swiping at the phone to try again. This time, the phone rang, crackled, and then a voice.

"Aaliyah!"

"Wade, I—" Aaliyah bit off her exclamation as she heard Wade continuing.

"—are—get to—area?" Wade's words were choppy and uninterpretable.

"Wade, I'm in a storage unit!" Aaliyah cried into the phone. As she did, she made her way across the unit to the door, trying to open it. It didn't budge. Whoever had locked her in must have padlocked it from the outside. If whoever had sequestered her here had brought her to Park Springs Storage Units, she would be easy to find. But if they'd transported her somewhere else outside of Park Springs, she could be anywhere. She could be deep on private lands in a private storage facility for all she knew.

"—hang on." Wade's voice cracked again.

"I don't know what unit I'm in!" She tried to communicate through the broken airwaves. "I'll keep my phone on!" Maybe they could ping her GPS coordinates based on her call. Triangulate it between cell towers.

Wade's voice broke through. "Stay put!"

Aaliyah couldn't help but release a watery, tear-filled laugh. Stay put. Where else would she go?

"Hurry!" she cried into the phone. For all she knew her abductor was returning in the next few moments. The killer—her *birth mother's* killer—would come back to finish what he'd started.

Why her? Because she'd discovered the dumping grounds of his victims, or worse? Was it possible that the killer was targeting her, toying with her even, because she was the daughter of Deborah Platt? All these years, Deborah had remained nameless until DNA had attached not only a name but genealogy to her. It had brought Wade—but how would the killer know anything about Aaliyah? He would have to have access to Wade's files. Or access to the case itself, wouldn't he? If he was targeting Aaliyah because of her relation to his first victim, then the killer was more integrated into the case than anyone had realized. Or else she had an overactive imagination.

Aaliyah leaned against the door, aching to have the strength or the know-how to break free from this prison. Her wrists and ankles were sore from being bound.

"God, I know You've promised to watch over me," she whispered. "Please don't forget that promise."

A tear slipped down her cheek, and she swiped it away. Every piece of her ached to believe, genuinely believe, that God would pull through for her. With her history of adoption, she'd always had that nagging sense that she'd been abandoned as a child. Now, with the latest information surrounding her birth and subsequent literal abandonment, her resolve to trust in anyone's faithfulness was delicate.

It seemed like hours, but the clanking of metal-on-metal finally startled Aaliyah from her prayers. She jumped away from the door.

"Wade?" she cried, before realizing it could very well be her abductor returning.

"Aaliyah?" Wade's voice broke through the crack between the door and its frame. "Hold on, we're coming!"

She heard him shout at someone to bring the bolt cutters. "Stand back." Wade's direction was easy to follow.

Aaliyah stepped back from the door and waited. Before she could try to calculate the amount of time she'd been trapped inside the storage unit, the door flung open and fresh air exploded against her face. Blue sky greeted her, and then a man's frame filled the doorway.

Without thinking, Aaliyah threw herself into Wade Marlowe's embrace. For a moment, they clung to each other, bound by the trauma of the last two days. She felt his hand against the small of her back, and his other hand held the back of her head with a gentle exploration of his fingers in her hair. She buried her face in his shoulder, breathing in the scent of security that was his smell.

"How did you find me?" Her words were muffled against his shirt.

"We were able to get your location from your phone. Buck remembered your mom has that app that tracks you."

"Go Mom," Aaliyah laughed, emotional and tired all the same.

"It didn't get us an exact location, but this was the most logical place for you to be stashed."

"Stashed?" Aaliyah pulled back, her smile lopsided. "I'm just inventory now?"

"I didn't mean it like that!" Wade's apology was fast, as though he wasn't sure if she truly was offended or not. Seeming to realize their intimate embrace, Wade dropped his arm, clearing his throat and running his palm along the back of his neck. Aaliyah stepped back. His dark eyes roved her face as he steered her from the unit.

Aaliyah noticed dust rising from the road just beyond.

More law enforcement was on its way. Wade Marlowe had beat them here. She took stock of her surroundings. This was not Park Springs Storage Units. It was an abandoned metal structure on public lands. There would be no way to tie it to anyone—to determine who had brought her here.

"Are you okay?" Wade's concern broke into Aaliyah's assessment.

"I-I'm fine." She put some distance between them as Buck's vehicle fishtailed down the gravel road.

"Did he hurt you?" Wade held her at arm's length, looking her up and down for injury.

"Not terribly." It was an understatement, Aaliyah realized. She'd been manhandled into unconsciousness, bound and left behind in a warehouse. Maybe the abductor had intended to just abandon her there, leaving her to starve until finally she died. Would he have tied an arrowhead bracelet on her wrist then? Found a new place to dump her body and recapture the euphoria he felt when burying a victim?

Aaliyah grappled for Wade's shirt sleeve. His eyes met hers. "Deborah Platt," she whispered hoarsely.

He frowned, scanning her face to interpret what she meant.

Aaliyah obliged him. "If Deborah Platt was his victim, why didn't he bury her like the others? Why wasn't she in the burial grounds I found in the Bob?"

"The evidence suggests she was his first victim," Wade provided.

"So then, he created the graves for the others *after* Deborah. She was—perhaps—his first taste of killing."

Wade nodded with affirmation, apparently not surprised by her deduction.

Aaliyah continued, forcing the words through her mouth. "So where was *I* when he killed her?"

"I'm not sure I'm following." The furrow between Wade's brows deepened.

"Did Deborah abandon me behind the old church, or..." Aaliyah's question seemed to sink in before she asked it, as realization spread across Wade's face.

"Or did the *Arrowhead Killer* leave you behind the church?" he finished for her.

Aaliyah wanted to believe that. For one wild and crazy moment, she wanted to believe the killer had done away with her birth mother and then been the one to get rid of her. It put her child abandonment on a different level than her birth mother simply refusing to have anything to do with her.

"He might have left you behind the church because he was conflicted. He couldn't kill an infant, and yet he didn't want you to live either. The church was a fifty-fifty chance you'd either perish or be found," Wade concluded the theory.

"And if the killer knows now that I'm still alive, *and* that I discovered his graveyard—" Aaliyah swallowed hard as she looked over Wade's shoulder to see Buck hurrying from his vehicle. She looked back at Wade. "He's still conflicted. He needs me out of his way. I'm a risk to him, to his identity."

"And yet he can't bring himself to end it." Wade nodded, a dark flicker of awareness in his eyes. "But how would he know you were Deborah's daughter? We've not made the DNA results public."

A tense silence hung between them. Only they knew, her parents, and Buck.

Wade spoke up. "Others have the read the case file. Back in Helena at the office. I mean, someone could have overheard in the station here in Park Springs."

"But if the Arrowhead Killer—as you call him—does know who I am, then according to this theory, I'm his first victim's child," Aaliyah stated.

"You're his first trophy from his first kill," Wade finished, "and now, you're also his biggest threat."

SIX

They had gotten off to a rotten start at no fault of anyone else but the Arrowhead Killer. Wade had a feeling in another time and place, and under completely different circumstances, he might have had one of those movie moments. Hero sees woman across the room. Woman's beauty knocks him senseless. Hero falls for the woman and immediately sets off to woo her.

Of course, this wasn't a sappy regency film, he wasn't wearing a cravat, and for all that was worth smiling at, he was no Mr. Darcy. He was simply Detective Wade Marlowe, attempting to make up for not being there for his sister when she'd been murdered and carrying his own baggage into a cold case that was opening up a bullet-point list of wounds for the woman he couldn't keep his eyes off.

Especially now.

Aaliyah Terrence sat across from him on a plaid wool blanket she'd spread on the grassy meadow by a stream that ran through Park Springs. Her coppery curls were loose about her shoulders, she wore a cream-colored blouse that made the freckles on her arms and cheeks more noticeable and more beautiful, and her jeans hugged her frame in just the right way. The two of them were sharing a picnic dessert, and they'd met on the outskirts of town. Dusk was settling in, bringing with it the slight chill of mountain air and the fresh scent of nature. With Glacier National Park not far away and the ever-growing city of Kalispell within easy driving distance, Park Springs felt like an oasis between nature's most remote beauty and humanity's doorway to the hustle and bustle.

But tonight? Tonight was a do-over. At least, Wade hoped it would be. With a full day to recuperate at her parents' ranch, Aaliyah had returned Wade's call and accepted his invitation. A simple dessert—he'd bring cheesecake or something from the local bakery—and some conversation under the expansive sky, and hopefully, they could connect on a level that wasn't under intense duress.

"Start over" were the words Wade had used, and he thought he'd been relatively successful in indicating that he meant nothing more than friendship. Did he want more? How could a man tell after two days of intense trauma? He just needed to meet Aaliyah Terrence on her turf, and somehow, he needed to separate her from the Arrowhead Killer if for no other reason than to understand more about her and her relationship to her past.

"You're awfully quiet for someone who wanted to get a restart," Aaliyah teased, and she took a bite of the strawberry cheesecake that balanced on a clear plastic plate on her knee.

Wade released a chuckle. "I guess I am."

Aaliyah adjusted her seat and set the plate aside, assessing him with those golden hazel eyes of hers. "We haven't had the chance to actually meet properly, Detective Marlowe." With a laugh, she stuck out her hand. "I'm Aaliyah Terrence, forest ranger in the Bob Marshall Wilderness. I have a dog named Peaches. I was adopted, and until a day or two ago, I believed it had been a fully normal adoption.

My parents own a small ranch. My godfather is the local sheriff. Cherry pie is my favorite dessert, and I embroider pillowcases when I'm bored."

That last declaration surprised Wade. "You embroider?"

Aaliyah nodded, picking at a leaf that stuck to her jeans. "I do. The residents at the local retirement home love an embroidered pillowcase, and it gives my hands something to do when my brain just needs to think. Give me a good French knot any day. They're so fun to make. It's quite satisfying."

Wade smiled, unsure how to transition the conversation to anything other than purely awkward or case centric.

"How about you?" Aaliyah smiled at him. "Aside from getting shot at, wrestling assailants and rescuing women locked in storage sheds, what do you do for fun?"

Wade released a full-on laugh. "That's quite the lead-in."

Aaliyah shrugged. "Hey. You couldn't ask for a more interesting introduction."

"True. I could've forgone the bullet though." Wade flexed his shoulder and was reminded of the graze on his bicep.

"Well?" Aaliyah tilted her head. "You came to Park Springs because of Deborah Platt's cold case. How did you get into solving cold cases?"

"I was assigned it," Wade answered, knowing there was more to the story.

"Sure." Aaliyah blinked in mock coquettishness. "And I was thrown into a truck and given a ranger's flat hat. C'mon. What drove you into law enforcement? You had to have an interest in it."

Wade glanced away. He let his gaze roam the horizon, the blue hills, the yellow meadow, the sky that had tiny stars beginning to twinkle. Amy. He rarely talked about his sister, but he supposed if he was going to get any honest information from Aaliyah about her upbringing, then he would have to give some about his.

He met her candid stare.

It was only fair.

"My sister."

Aaliyah's expression grew somber. "I'm so sorry. I—wasn't thinking when I asked you that." She reached out and touched the back of his hand with her fingertips. Though she didn't leave her fingers there, he felt the imprint of them all the same.

"I always blamed myself for not being there for Amy—for not protecting her." Okay, he was getting too vulnerable too quick. "I was already in law enforcement, so when the opportunity came to investigate cold cases and I could get justice for the families of other murder victims, I took it." There. The fast answer was far safer.

Aaliyah drew in an unsteady breath and turned her own eyes toward the horizon. "I always knew I was adopted. I had no clue that I was the daughter of the unknown victim that's haunted this place since I can remember. It's so surreal, and now..." Her voice trailed off, and her words left them both hanging right in the present circumstances Wade wished they could leave behind.

On impulse, he reached for her hand and was admittedly surprised when Aaliyah curled her fingers around his instead of pulling away. "I never meant my arrival in Park Springs to be nearly this traumatizing for you."

There it was. That was the guilt he was feeling. He wanted to protect her, the way he should have protected Amy, but in the last forty-eight hours, all he'd succeeded in doing was adding exclamation points to the already volatile circumstances Aaliyah had found herself in.

"What are the odds the day you arrived in town to reveal my birth mother was Deborah Platt, would also be the day my dog happens upon what is probably her killer's sacred burial site for his other victims?" Aaliyah's tone held irony, if not a watery laugh.

Wade wondered if she was more emotional than she let on. It wouldn't surprise him in the slightest if she were upset and frightened, covering it with a nonchalant exterior. He didn't press her, but instead responded carefully. "I guess sometimes when God allows one domino to fall, He lets the others start toppling with it." Wade squeezed Aaliyah's fingers. "We'll get to the bottom of the Arrowhead Killer. I promise."

"You can't promise something you can't control." Aaliyah pulled her hand from his, and Wade felt an instant barrier build between them. She eyed him cautiously. "People make promises all the time, and then they abandon their promises."

Wade could tell that was her experience speaking. And how could he blame her? The revelation of her adoption circumstances was wild enough, let alone finding out her adoptive parents and godfather, Buck—the sheriff, for that matter—had covered it all up as a normal adoption process.

"My parents always told me I had sealed adoption records, and someday they'd help me get them unsealed. That's a promise that will never be fulfilled." Aaliyah grimaced. "Now they're trying to make up for it—desperately."

Wade had wondered how the previous night and day had been for Aaliyah, seeing as Buck had insisted she not return alone to her house. She'd relocated to her parents' ranch with Peaches. It had to be tense and emotional there considering the recent revelations.

Aaliyah took another bite of her cheesecake as though

she needed something to do while she considered her next words. Wade allowed her the silence. Sometimes people were more apt to talk—to *trust*—when not feeling interrogated.

He was right.

Aaliyah swallowed and released a small sigh. "I don't know exactly how my adoption was considered legal—or if it was. I have a birth certificate, I have a social security number, so I know my parents managed it somehow. But the circumstances? They finally told me a pastor found me as a baby behind the Park Springs Church and brought me to the police station. Buck took me to my parents because he needed someone to watch me and because he knew they'd already been looking into adoption. The rest was history. Handled quietly and off the record. The local news never even knew about my story. People just knew that somehow my parents had worked with an agency to adopt a baby, and here I was."

"You weren't turned in to social services?" Wade had a challenging time believing it had all been that simple not to mention subtle.

Aaliyah frowned. "My parents were already certified foster parents. CPS had no issue with me being placed with them as an infant, which then led to my subsequent adoption."

"I still don't get how no one heard about an abandoned baby in a small town." Wade couldn't help his skepticism. Something about it was still off. "Did your parents tell you when the pastor found you behind the church?" Wade already knew, but he was curious if Aaliyah had been told the same story. If the story was consistent, it was a sign that they were being told the truth. But if it was too consistent—as in scripted—then he would begin to suspect a deeper sort of cover-up.

Aaliyah's expression was disappointed. She reached for a stick that lay by her feet and snapped it in two. "They said he found me in the early evening. When he turned me in, he kept it confidential when asked."

It matched.

"That pastor has long since left Park Springs, so now the only ones locally involved with my adoption are Buck and my parents. Gordon didn't even know about me."

Gordon. Buck's brother, Aaliyah's coworker. Wade reminded himself of the connections. "And what about your neighbor—Charlie Beedle?"

Aaliyah's eyes snapped up to meet his. "Are you still suspicious of Charlie?" Her voice went up in pitch and irritation.

Wade held up his hands. "Hey, I'm just trying to connect all the dots. The killer has obviously been around for a long time. I need to know anyone who might have connections to you and then, potentially, to Deborah Platt."

"Deborah Platt was a transient, Buck said. She was in town and then she was gone, and no one wondered. Besides," she leveled a glare at him, "Park Springs isn't the only town in these parts. Who's to say the Arrowhead Killer is a local? The Bob Marshall Wilderness is a huge expanse. Just because the graves were found where they were doesn't mean the killer is from the area. They could be from Kalispell or Seeley Lake or even Missoula. Why narrow your investigation into Park Springs?"

"Because." Wade hated to be this direct, but she hadn't left him much choice. "You're right. Deborah Platt *was* a drifter. From the records I can find, she was in Park Springs for about ten months and then she disappeared. She didn't have any friends here. She waitressed at the diner on Sixth Street and Tenth Avenue and lived a good majority of her time at the local shelter. No one cared when she came, and no one cared when she vanished. I'm going to guess if we get solid identification on the other victims, they'll come back as transient women too."

He noted the wince that crossed Aaliyah's face, and he felt the same pang also. Sometimes society overlooked people who deserved more than that. Wade cleared his throat to continue.

"With Deborah's body having been found not buried, plus the fact she wore the telltale arrowhead bracelet, that suggests she was the killer's first victim. He didn't have a place to hide the body. He wasn't established enough. The other victims probably aren't from Park Springs. *They're* the ones who are likely from other places, and he brought them to the Bob to dispose of them. Which means Park Springs and victim number one—your birth mother—were the epicenter. It all started here."

"And somehow I survived," Aaliyah concluded.

"So what was—what *is*—the killer's tie to you?" Wade asked the inevitable question—the one they had already flirted with the day before.

Aaliyah's sniff of disbelief surprised Wade, and he brought his eyes up to meet hers. She gave him a sad smile. "So much for a do-over," she stated. "I guess we're bound to be tied together by murder."

Wade winced. That was the last thing he had hoped for, and the only thing worse would be if he couldn't protect Aaliyah from what he knew was still looming in the shadows. All the unanswered questions were going to demand a conclusion, and Wade promised himself he would be there when the conclusion came. He wouldn't let happen to Aaliyah what he had let happen to his sister.

Aaliyah would live.

Aaliyah wished she could be warmer, more inviting. She'd tried. A few minutes ago, she'd almost felt flirtatious with the good-looking detective and his five-o'clock shadow that traced his jawline. Instead, she'd been overwhelmed again by the events of the past few days. What she hadn't told Wade—because it was none of his business—was that she had avoided her parents with the immaturity of a teenage girl avoiding conflict. She had no desire to try to rectify the tension between them. There was no justification they could give her that would adequately explain away the deceit of keeping her adoptive circumstances so secret. And why the secrets? Had they been afraid the birth mother would reappear and claim her? They certainly couldn't have known when Deborah Platt's unidentified body was found that *she* was Aaliyah's mother. Unless, of course, they'd had suspicions—gut instincts—hence the secrets.

Aaliyah allowed herself to squash the tempestuous emotions boiling inside of her. She was an emotional wreck, if she were honest. She was scared, she was angry, she was frightened that the Arrowhead Killer seemed to have placed a bull's-eye on her and yet—not that she wanted him to—also didn't seem excited to kill her. He was resorting to a sort of psychological mind game and physical attacks that didn't let her forget he was there, looming in the shadows.

Wade cleared his throat, and it broke Aaliyah's silent musings. She met his dark eyes. What had happened to his sister? The circumstances around her murder? A piece of Aaliyah ached for Wade, and another piece of her regretted her words the first day they'd met when she'd claimed he didn't understand what it was to be on the victim's side.

He did understand.

It was what made Wade Marlowe the man he was.

Aaliyah managed a small smile even as she was forced to admit to herself that she liked the man he was. She liked his strength, his gentle respect of her, his protective nature and the fact that he didn't force conversation.

The stars were out in full brilliance now, with dusk having melted into the night sky. She'd have to go back to her parents' ranch soon, sneak in and hide in her room like a chastised child. She had no desire to do that.

"Well, well," a voice broke into their tentative silence. "Trying to find a moment of peace?"

Aaliyah startled until she recognized Gordon approaching them in the darkness. He was out of his ranger uniform and dressed in his typical blue jeans and T-shirt. His graying hair was ruffled, and he held his hands lazily at his waist, thumbs hooked through the belt loops on his jeans.

Wade shifted and extended his hand up to shake Gordon's. "*Trying to* is the key phrase there," he admitted.

Gordon exchanged an empathetic look with Aaliyah, and he crouched down to their level so they didn't feel him looming over them. "Yeah, it's been a crazy last couple of days."

"I'll be back to work on Thursday," Aaliyah reassured him.

Gordon waved her off. "You take care of you. There are other rangers, we can spread out the workload." He shifted his attention to Wade. "My brother said it'll quiet down soon anyway. They've removed the remains and processed the area. Besides, there are thousands of acres in the Bob.

I'm going to guess whoever was sick enough to bury their victims where you found them has moved on by now."

Aaliyah winced. While Gordon was right, it wasn't comforting to think of the killer finding a new place in the wilderness to continue his body burials. That meant he wasn't finished taking victims.

"On one hand, having him move on would be a relief." Wade nodded toward Aaliyah, but his expression was somber. "But we know he hasn't."

Gordon grimaced and raked his fingers through his hair. "Yeah. Guess you're right. Well, you stay safe, kiddo. I'll cover for you with rangers—and talk to the supervisor." He wagged his finger at Aaliyah. "You just make sure when you do come back you check in with me at the station. I need to know where you are always. If something happened to you, Buck would kill me."

Aaliyah managed a small laugh. She wasn't Gordon's responsibility. She wasn't Buck's either. In reality, she was her own responsibility, so staying safe and playing it smart was going to be key.

Gordon bid them farewell and continued his own nighttime walk. He hadn't left them alone for more than a few minutes when Aaliyah's phone trilled in her pocket.

"I better check this." She tossed Wade an apologetic look. She had a feeling tonight wasn't as relaxed as he'd hoped it would be. If this was supposed to have been a date, they'd both done an abysmal job of leaving the events of the week behind them.

She didn't recognize the number, but the phone lit up the space between them on the blanket. Aaliyah shot a look at Wade, a disconcerting feeling jumping in her stomach.

"I don't know who it is."

"Put it on speaker," he advised.

Aaliyah did so. "Hello?"

There was silence on the other end.

"Hello?" she tried again.

"It's you." The voice was a whisper. A hiss really. Indistinguishable as anything familiar.

Her hand tightened on her phone, and Aaliyah couldn't peel her eyes from the lit screen that stared back at her with the chilling identification of Unknown Number.

"Who are you?" she asked, trying to squelch the quiver in her voice. She could feel the memory of her assailant's strength, both in her house and the feed lot where his arm had slid around her neck.

"I didn't know who you were." Another drawn-out sentence with the words half sung in a whispered taunt. "But now I do."

"Tell me who you are!" Aaliyah cried into the phone, her hand trembling to the point she could barely hold on to it.

Wade's fingers curled around her wrist. He carefully extricated the phone from her grasp and gave her fingers a reassuring squeeze.

"Detective Marlowe here. Identify yourself," Wade commanded.

There was a hiss on the other end of the line, as though whoever it was pushed aggravated breath through their teeth.

The line went dead.

SEVEN

"There's no way to trace the call." Buck paced the parking lot at the edge of the park. Crickets chirruped in the bushes, protected by the night's darkness and oblivious to the fear that left Aaliyah leaning against her truck, hugging her arms around herself.

Wade had called Buck the moment Aaliyah's mysterious caller had hung up. The sheriff had wasted no time in coming to meet them, even though Wade had suggested they meet at the station.

Now the men paced the small, remote lot of the little park, and the darkness enveloped them. It was strange how a blanket of black could leave her feeling so exposed, while the daylight that lifted the curtain of night and revealed the world seemed so much more comforting. It was the darkness that hid evil. And that was what this was. It was evil.

Aaliyah wrapped her arms around herself and leaned against Buck's car. She wasn't safe in her home. She wasn't safe in town. And she wasn't safe in a park with a detective from law enforcement. Wherever she went, *he* was going to find her. The Arrowhead Killer. Somehow—some way—he had assumed a connection to her.

"He said he knows who you are now." Wade's restatement of the caller's claim didn't help Aaliyah's nerves.

"Meaning what? That I'm Deborah Platt's abandoned baby all grown up?" She voiced their earlier suspicions aloud, glancing at Buck, who didn't meet her eyes. "And how would he know that?" Aaliyah knew she was treading into uncharted territory. She was all but questioning Buck without asking the question blatantly.

Buck's expression was shuttered. "If that's what he meant, then how he found out is a mystery."

"It means someone on the inside leaked the information about Aaliyah's DNA connection to Deborah Platt." Wade's declaration sent a tingling chill up Aaliyah's spine.

She hugged herself tighter, wishing she could relish the soft night breeze that whisper-kissed her face, or enjoy the distant rippling sound of the creek and focus in on the far off yapping of the coyotes. Instead, Aaliyah directed her attention to Wade, making out his worried expression that was highlighted by the glow of the parking lot's light.

Aaliyah wasn't sure what was worse. The idea that Buck was somehow untrustworthy—even involved at some level—or that someone else with access to the information had an unknown motive that targeted her. She eyed Buck, finding herself taking a step closer to Wade. How she hated it—this doubting her godfather. Doubting his honesty.

"I didn't share any of the case with anyone that wasn't authorized." Buck met Aaliyah's look with a frank one of his own that seemed to beg her to trust him.

She looked away.

"I've been on the phone with my department back in Helena." Wade directed his statement to Buck, but Aaliyah noticed he was carefully watching Buck's reaction. It seemed Buck noticed Wade's scrutiny too. He raised an eyebrow as Wade continued.

"I've got a buddy there that's helping me profile the Arrowhead Killer to see if we can get into his head. Deborah's sister, Lori, indicated that Deborah had disappeared for months at a time, and often the family just let her be. But I have another call in to her—I want to ask more questions about what she may still know. Any connections Deborah may have had in the area that she may have told Lori about before she died. Who may have had an opportunity to kill her?"

Buck shifted his weight to another foot.

Aaliyah had watched too many crime shows. She was immediately suspicious that Buck was edgy—nervous even. Then she realized he may very well have just been getting more comfortable. She needed to stop this! There was no way that Buck of all people had anything to do with the events of the last couple of days. The only thing he was guilty of was hiding details about her adoption—and some would probably make the argument he'd done that to protect her.

"I'm building a list of names of the people who may have crossed paths with Deborah here in Park Springs before she died." Wade's conclusion drew Aaliyah back to the current conversation.

Buck blew out a hefty breath. "I'll see what more I can dig up too, now that we've identified Deborah."

"Good." Wade's tone grew stern. "Her sister said she stayed at the shelter. She worked at a diner. That much Lori could supply me with. So it means that someone around Park Springs knew her—probably knew her better than we're crediting them. They've kept silent all these years, or assumed Deborah just moved on. But we know better now. I think it's time we release the name of Park Springs's unknown murder victim to the press so we can glean more information."

Aaliyah met Wade's eyes. There was something in his that left her feeling vulnerable and raw. His next words confirmed her fears. "If the Arrowhead Killer claims to have identified *you*, Aaliyah, then keeping the story under lock and key isn't going to aid the investigation or offer you any protection," Wade confirmed. "We need people who might have information to step forward."

Buck growled and kicked at the car's tire.

"What?" Aaliyah didn't know if it was because her nerves were so on edge or because her mind was foggy with fear, but she felt like the two men had concluded something she wasn't following.

"What's wrong?" Aaliyah was at a loss. "We already determined the killer knows my name, and that he's figured out I'm Deborah Platt's daughter."

"Right." Buck's words were forced through a resigned sigh. He met Aaliyah's eyes. "Which means if we go public with Deborah's identity, you'll get drawn into the limelight at some point. Not to mention, it could make the killer more desperate to shut you up."

Aaliyah eyed Buck as the sheriff propped his hands at his waist. He was in his sixties, but he was strong, and he was more agitated than she'd seen him before.

He continued. "I want this treated with kid gloves, Marlowe. If you're going to the press with this information."

Wade summarized the situation in a clipped tone. "Before I do, we need to clarify who knew I was coming to Park Springs as a result of Deborah's identity being determined through DNA. We need to zero in on who would be close enough to the case to know that DNA has linked Aaliyah to Deborah as her child. And then we need to review those people to see who would be familiar enough with the wilderness to bury other victims there. What links them to these other victims? What do they have in common with Deborah Platt, and how does that tie to the killer?"

Aaliyah's head was spinning, and she felt her legs begin to shake. She slid down the side of the car into a squatting position in the parking lot.

Buck bent beside her, reaching for her shoulder. "Aaliyah?" Worry laced his voice.

She pulled away from him, but she was fast enough to catch the glimmer of hurt cross his face.

Wade joined them, crouching in front of her, his soft gaze claiming hers, urging her silently to trust him. To listen to him. "We're going to keep you safe," he reassured her, although it only went so far. "We need to connect the dots. Until then, you cannot be alone."

"I'm staying with Mom and Dad."

"That's good," Wade inserted. "But I'm meaning anywhere you go. I don't want you to be alone."

"I have Peaches. I'll bring her with me." Aaliyah preferred Peaches for company anyway. The dog was comforting, and she eased Aaliyah's nerves.

"I'm sure Peaches would do her best to protect you." Wade reached out, and his fingers grazed Aaliyah's cheek. She looked up at him, startled by the tender and familiar gesture. He softened his voice. "But you need to be with me." And then, as the words filled the air between them, Wade's eyes widened as though he realized how assumptive he sounded, and also how intimate the moment had become. The air was thick between them, but Buck was there too. Even now, he cleared his throat. Wade added quickly, "Or you need to be with one of the local authorities."

Aaliyah noted Wade hadn't specified Buck. She searched his face, but there was nothing there to confirm he too was suspicious of how much Buck knew.

The moment dissipated as quickly as it'd built. Wade adjusted his footing as he continued to crouch on the ground next to Aaliyah and Buck. He directed his attention to the sheriff. "And, lastly, we need to go back to the scene." Wade's declaration was unexpected.

Aaliyah stared at him. "You mean—"

"We might have missed something at or around the burial site that would help us figure out who this creep is." Wade's statement was met with Buck's snort of disbelief.

"With the amount of investigators that have been combing the area the last few days, what do you think you'll find that they didn't?"

Aaliyah felt like she was watching a ping-pong match between the two men.

Wade shrugged. "I don't know. Maybe nothing. But Aaliyah hasn't revisited the area since she found it. Going there might trigger a memory. Or maybe she'll see something connected to that first attack that she's simply not recalling now."

"You want to take *Aaliyah* back to the crime scene?" Buck's incredulous tone was bordering on anger.

Aaliyah pushed back against the vehicle and rose on shaky feet. "I'll go." Her determination was wrapped in her own fear. But this wasn't going to go away. *He* wasn't going to go away. And it had become much more personal than her stumbling over a killer's graveyard. The killer was attached to her because she was tied to his victim. His first victim. Perhaps even the trophy victim that had started his spree of killing and by whom he measured each subsequent murder. "Whatever I need to do—" Aaliyah prayed silently for courage "—I'll do it. I want this to end."

She wanted answers. She wanted to know why Deborah Platt—or whoever—had dumped her behind the church as an infant. She wanted to know why the killer had murdered Deborah, leaving her body exposed but potentially identifiable at the time. She wanted to know why he'd continued to kill, and then why, in an ironic turn, he'd chosen to bury his victims in the wilderness Aaliyah saw as her refuge. The Bob Marshall Wilderness was expansive. Thousands of acres. Miles of wilderness, much of which one couldn't get to except on horseback. It couldn't be coincidental that the Arrowhead Killer had buried his victims in an area that was accessible by campers and rangers. It was almost as though, the last twenty years, the Arrowhead Killer *wanted* to be discovered.

Aaliyah nodded, not quite believing what she was going to say. "Maybe if I go back, I'll see something that can help us figure out who the Arrowhead Killer is. We could retrace my steps for that entire day. The Bob's gravesite region, head back to my place where the guy broke into my house, and even go back to the warehouse."

"Aaliyah." Buck stated her name in such a way that made Aaliyah feel if she pushed forward with the idea, she'd make Buck angry.

"I can't just wait for him to come to me," Aaliyah argued. She straightened her shoulders, willing her stubbornness to become stronger than her fear. "He needs to be stopped so I can carry on with my life. So his victims can get justice. So Deborah Platt—" She cut off her words and glanced at Wade. "So my birth mother can rest in peace."

Buck took a few steps toward her, then stopped. The lines in his eyes were deep with worry, and he lifted his hand as if to reach for her, but he dropped it to his side instead. "If Deborah Platt were here now, she would ask you to leave it to the authorities to figure this out, to keep you safe. That's probably why she left you behind the church as a baby. Not to abandon you to the elements, but—to pray that God saw fit to have someone find you. Protect you." Buck's voice choked with emotion. "And that's what your parents and I did."

Aaliyah blinked rapidly as tears welled in her eyes. Maybe Buck was right. Maybe he and her parents, by making her adoption appear normal and from outside of Park Springs, had diverted attention and publicity away from her as the little abandoned church baby. But maybe, in their attempt to protect her from the sensationalism of her story, they had merely delayed the inevitable.

She was, as Deborah Platt's infant daughter, a loose end of the Arrowhead Killer's first victim. He may not have known about her before, but now he did.

"Let him come," Aaliyah whispered to herself.

"What was that?" Buck's eyebrow rose.

Aaliyah directed her gaze straight at the man. "I said, 'Let him come.'"

Wade could tell Aaliyah wasn't sleeping well. There were shadows under her eyes, and as she climbed into the passenger side of his rented truck a few days later, she let out an audible sigh.

"Bad night?" he asked with a sideways glance as he pulled away from her parents' ranch.

Aaliyah nodded but didn't elaborate.

The last day or two had been suspiciously uneventful, which was nice on the one hand. He'd been able to do some digging and collect some names of people in Park Springs who may have interacted with Deborah Platt twenty-five years ago. He'd chatted with Deborah Platt's sister, Lori, again. Though she hadn't had much more to add, there were a few leads worth checking into. And his pal back in

Helena had developed a profile on the Arrowhead Killer. A profile that was leaving Wade searching for the right time to expose it to Aaliyah. It was disturbing, but she deserved to know.

At least Aaliyah's phone had been silent, with no unidentified calls. Her house remained untouched from what they could see when they'd dropped in to collect a few more of her things. After the initial surge of attacks and stalking, the perpetrator had gone horribly silent.

The only thing worse than a violent and unpredictable enemy was a calculated and silent one.

Wade preferred the Arrowhead Killer when he was acting impulsively and giving the impression he was heavily influenced by emotional reactions. But now, the lack of activity over the last forty-eight hours told Wade that the killer was also capable of stepping away from his emotion and recalibrating. Because, Wade knew, the killer had not been frightened off. That wasn't the killer's MO.

He cleared his throat. There was never going to be a *right time*. "So, I talked to my buddy Eric—the one who works in homicide and does profiling. I got his take about our killer's profile."

Aaliyah's head twisted. As Wade drove, he could feel her eyes drilling into him.

"And?" she asked. "What'd he say?"

"There were a few things he pointed out. The fact that the Arrowhead Killer has flown under the radar for twenty-five years and only has five victims, to the best of our knowledge, tells him that the killer isn't out for attention. He's not following his crimes in the media or glorying in tripping up the authorities."

"*Only* five?" Aaliyah's tone indicated there were already too many bodies.

Wade didn't want to expand on the fact some serial killers made a sport of it and had body counts in the double digits. "Five victims over a quarter of a century? Either he's a far more prolific killer with other burial sites, or he's extremely self-controlled and calculated. His kills have a reason behind them. They're not just random opportunities, but he takes the opportunity to act out something that suits a narrative he's concocted."

"That's just creepy." Aaliyah's voice was small. Wade had to agree. "Eric said that now that you uncovered the Arrowhead Killer's victims, and we've identified the connection to Deborah via the arrowhead bracelets left on all the victims, he wants the credit. Not the fame or glory, but he wants us to know they're his. It's possessiveness. He wants to claim them, and he wants to claim you as his."

"You're kidding." Aaliyah visibly shrank back into her seat.

Wade adjusted his grip on the steering wheel. "You're more than a loose end, Aaliyah. You're part of Deborah. You're part of the woman he killed, which means he thinks you also belong to him." Wade's words dissipated as though he didn't want to finish his thought. "Eric said the killer may want to relive it again, to capture the euphoria that first stalk and kill brought to him. To claim the final piece of Deborah Platt."

"So he's a bona fide sociopath?" Aaliyah stated as the truck bounced over a pothole in the road.

"The Arrowhead Killer?" Wade clarified unnecessarily. He knew who Aaliyah referred to. "No. If anything, he's a psychopath."

"Aren't they the same thing?" She quirked an eyebrow.

"The terms are interchanged a lot, but they have differences. Sociopaths don't care about others' feelings. They can be hotheaded, erratic, antisocial. They can even make excuses for their actions because they can recognize the impact or error of their decisions. A psychopath, frankly, is more calculated. They put on the act that they're caring, they build relationships even if they're not real ones, and they can even have affection in their own way. They're not necessarily antisocial and awkward, and they have zero remorse for their actions—although they may pretend that they do."

"And you don't think this guy is impulsive and hotheaded?" Aaliyah sounded doubtful.

Wade adjusted his grip on the steering wheel, flicking his left turn signal. "Eric says no. He said that even though the last few days make it seem like he is, the fact he's played it so carefully the last twenty-some years, and the fact he's pulled back now and gone silent, says otherwise. He's thinking things through. Weighing his next action and probably identifying how he hurt himself by going after you three different times."

"That's not comforting." Aaliyah reached back and lifted red curls from her shoulders, twisting them into a messy bun at the nape of her neck. "And I need to get back to work. I can't just ride around with you and hope someone doesn't kill me."

"Why not?" Wade steered the truck into a parking spot along a side street just outside the diner where Deborah Platt had once worked so many years before. He wasn't trying to aggravate Aaliyah, but truth be told, if she were killed, what good would her job as a ranger be?

"Because that's not realistic. Besides, Gordon will be there. My supervisors check in. I'm not alone all the time and after this, Gordon will watch me like a hawk. Buck might be my godfather, but it's almost like Gordon is godfather number two, and I'm sandwiched between two crusty bachelors who really need lives beyond me and this town."

Wade stopped the engine and raised his eyebrows at Aaliyah. "Well, the fact is, we have people to talk to about Deborah and what happened back then, and I'd like to have you along."

Aaliyah followed his motion and climbed from the truck. As she shut the door, she eyed him over the hood. "How does me coming with you help?"

He debated only a moment before opting for blatant honesty. "People are more likely to remember when there's something on the line. We're about to release it to the press anyway now that I've gotten a few things followed up on. If we let people know you just found out you're Deborah Platt's daughter, they'll probably take our questions more seriously."

"And the fact Deborah was murdered isn't enough motivation?" Aaliyah slung her day pack over her shoulder to follow Wade to the diner.

"That was over two decades ago. People forget."

"Well, obviously the Arrowhead Killer hasn't." Aaliyah's declaration was the punctuation on the end of their conversation.

"I was forty-two that year." Judy Stillwater sat across from Wade and Aaliyah in one of the diner's booths. The seat, upholstered in teal Naugahyde, squeaked beneath Judy as she adjusted her position.

Aaliyah's leg brushed against Wade's, and though he didn't react, she jerked hers away. The very feel of his muscled leg against hers inspired an emotion she didn't want to analyze. Attraction? Absolutely. A desire to be closer, to lean into the strength his body exuded? Yes.

Yep. She needed to stop thinking of Wade Marlowe's leg and focus on Judy Stillwater's recollection of Deborah Platt.

Judy's graying-blond, shoulder-length hair was pulled back in a low pony. She wore the stereotypical garb of a waitress in a diner, complete with the starched blue dress and white apron. There was a softness to her face, and while a few wrinkles around her eyes and lips tried to reveal her age, Judy was holding her own while she trudged toward seventy years of age.

"How well did you know Deborah?" Wade asked, his elbows on the table, his fingers steepled.

"Oh," Judy clicked her tongue, "no one knew Deborah well. She was so private. Never talked much. She never even mentioned where she was from originally."

"Did she have anyone she hung out with after work? Anyone who would pick her up or drop her off?"

Judy squinted as if trying to travel back in her memories. "She was picked up once or twice, I think, but I don't know who it was. Unfortunate thing was so pregnant." Judy offered Aaliyah the type of pitying smile that made Aaliyah squirm. "Who would've known she was pregnant with *you*? Aaliyah Terrence. When your mama and dad adopted you, they were so proud."

"And you didn't know that the Terrences' new infant was Deborah's child?" Wade's line of questioning was brutal to Aaliyah's emotions.

Aaliyah swallowed hard, paying close attention to the metal spoon she toyed with.

Judy shook her head. "We had no reason to wonder. Deborah disappeared about as unceremoniously as she'd first come. Here one day, gone the next. You know the type."

"You didn't try to find her?" Wade was relentless, but Judy didn't seem to take offense.

"Oh, we called around, sure. I checked with the shelter. They said she'd packed up her things and left and—well, what were we supposed to do? We didn't know anyone to call, and if she wanted to move on, then, she was an adult. I had no idea she'd given birth to you, Aaliyah." Judy's gaze fell back on Aaliyah, and Aaliyah tried to smile politely and not squirm beneath the sympathy in Judy's eyes. Judy shifted her attention back to Wade and straightened in her seat. "See, Park Springs is a small town and all, Detective, but we mind our own business when we should. And everyone who knew the Terrences knew they were trying to adopt long before Deborah showed up, so I wouldn't have had the slightest inclination to connect their new baby—Aaliyah—with Deborah Platt. I figured they finally drew the golden ticket with their adoption agency."

"And when the body was found? You didn't wonder if it was Deborah?" Wade had yet to look friendly at Judy. He was impassive. Serious.

Judy didn't seem swayed. "Detective, do you know how many missing persons posters hang on the telephone poles? Sure, I wondered. I wondered if it was her, I wondered if it was any one of the strangers passing through that I've served here in the diner. There was nothing to suggest that woman was Deborah. No more than that dead woman was someone I knew! Deborah had already been gone for well over a month or two by then."

"And the arrowhead bracelet?" Wade led.

Aaliyah eyed him. Hadn't that part been left out of the papers and public knowledge?

Judy offered him a blank look. "What arrowhead bracelet?"

"Never mind." Wade smiled then, his features warming.

"You've been helpful. I thank you." He extended his hand, and they shook, both rising to their feet.

Judy reached for Aaliyah to give her a swift embrace. Aaliyah accepted it awkwardly. She knew Judy from the diner, but she'd never felt any kinship with her. Now it seemed a bit forced, and Aaliyah drew back from the hug with a shaky smile.

"If I had known…" Judy patted Aaliyah's arm, and her expression had yet to change from the pitiable sad look that unnerved her.

As Aaliyah exited the diner behind Wade, she expelled a breath of relief, her eyes drinking in the distant hills that abutted against the broad map of blue sky.

"You okay?" Wade paused, eyeing her.

Aaliyah nodded. "I'm fine," she answered. But it wasn't the entire truth. The more she chewed on Judy's memories of Deborah Platt, the more real Deborah became to Aaliyah. Deborah Platt had been a young, single pregnant woman passing through a town that, in truth, made little effort to embrace her into their circle. Deborah had been alone, then at some point, she'd given birth, and then…she'd been murdered and forgotten.

Aaliyah climbed into Wade's truck but bit her lower lip as she turned to stare out the window. She was all that remained of Deborah Platt. She was the abandoned legacy of a woman who, without modern science, would have slipped into oblivion forever. The first of several who vanished from their family trees at the hand of a killer whose reason for murdering them seemed to be…what? To quench a lust for death? Or was it, as Wade's profiler friend said, the need to recapture the fulfillment he'd felt when he'd finally snuffed life from Deborah Platt? He saw Deborah as his—the victims following were sad attempts to recreate her—and now? Now he had his sights on Aaliyah.

She was Deborah's daughter, and the Arrowhead Killer meant to reenact his final scene with Aaliyah as his leading lady.

EIGHT

They had spent all yesterday interviewing the individuals that Buck had identified as those who may still remember Deborah Platt. Judy had been the first. Then a long-time staff member at the shelter where Deborah had periodically been known to stay. They had been no more helpful than Judy had. Wade had insisted on visiting Charlie again, but this time, Aaliyah refused to accompany him. She had no intention of making dear old Charlie feel even the slightest bit like a suspect again. All these years later, the old man was the best neighbor that Aaliyah could ask for—not to mention the baked goods. So she'd convinced Wade that she would be fine at her place across the road while he talked to Charlie.

The conversation must have shed no further light on anything, because Wade returned to Aaliyah's with a thoughtful expression and nothing else to add. Now it was a new day, and when she'd met Wade for coffee that morning, Wade had given her a quick update as to what she had missed after returning to her parents' ranch yesterday afternoon.

"I tried to get a hold of the pastor who originally found you as an infant behind the church." Wade's announcement didn't surprise Aaliyah. That was a logical person to pursue. "And I contacted the local medical clinic here in Park Springs in hopes of getting some record of Deborah Platt having checked in there for prenatal care. They didn't give me anything, and without a subpoena, I'm at a loss there. Same with the hospital in Kalispell."

After coffee, Wade finally suggested that today be the day they head out to the Bob and the burial grounds Aaliyah had stumbled on just a little over a week ago now.

"Today?" She had felt braver the other night when Wade made the suggestion that they revisit the graves. Now Aaliyah was finding herself a bit of glutton to maintain the thin thread of peace she'd found for the moment.

"Are we waiting for something?" Wade challenged.

"No, I just—" Aaliyah cut off her excuse. "No. You're right. We should go."

The more days that went by with silence from the Arrowhead Killer, the more tempted she was to be lulled into complacent awareness. But no. He was still there. She could sense him just off in the shadows, brewing his next move, taunting her with his quiet observation. It wouldn't do to pretend they were on a relaxed investigation of a cold case from twenty-five years ago. That case had merged with the present. And she was dead center in that present.

Staying at her parents' ranch was taking its toll too. Her mom was suffocating her with longing looks that begged Aaliyah to talk to them. To forgive them. To try to bridge the gap that had formed between them since Aaliyah had found out about the deception surrounding her adoption.

Now? She made the dumbest suggestion of her life.

"We should stop by my parents' ranch first." She'd said it before she'd thought through the implications. Being away from the ranch during the day allowed her to easily avoid her parents and the inevitable conversations. But their need for day packs and proper supplies before they headed out on the gravel roads into the Bob Marshall Wilderness had spurred Aaliyah to suggest getting them from the ranch. She had a few go-packs already prepped there as her parents' ranch was on the route to the Bob. But now she wished she'd kept her mouth shut. They could have just as easily stopped at the ranger station. Gordon would have supplies there, and he would've been able to prep exactly what they would need.

It was too late now.

Aaliyah winced as she hiked up the steps to the log house, Wade on her heels and Peaches on the porch wagging her tail in greeting. Behind Peaches were her parents, stationed at the door like guards who had no intention of allowing Aaliyah to sneak by them this time. Her mom had the worst expression of hurt and regret on her face, and it dug at Aaliyah's core even while she grew tense with the ongoing sense of betrayal.

Wade's hand touched the small of her back. "Let's do this." His gentle prod was to encourage her to stay the course. Now wasn't the time for a family showdown. They stopped at the ranch to get supplies. Water bottles, a sat phone, her bear spray…all the things they'd need to be smart when heading into the Bob. And Peaches. Of course she wanted to pick up her dog.

"Aaliyah, we'd like to talk." Her dad stood with arms crossed over his short-sleeved plaid Western shirt. His boots were caked in dried dirt, his jeans stained with evidence of ranch life.

"Not now, please." Aaliyah had to remind herself she was a grown woman. It'd be easier to rebuff her dad if he didn't look so intensely regretful.

He stepped in front of her to thwart her charge into the house. "Please."

Aaliyah stopped, sensing Wade close behind her. The warmth of his body and the strength that emanated from his presence boosted her resolve. "Now isn't the time, Dad."

"We're worried about you." Her mother's voice made her breath hitch. Aaliyah avoided her gaze.

"I know." Aaliyah glanced at Wade. "But—this is Detective Marlowe, from Helena. We—we're heading out to the Bob, and we need to get going."

"Mr. Terrence." Wade extended his hand to Aaliyah's dad. A strong, hearty shake was exchanged, but there was also a thick line of tension that enveloped the four of them as they all stood on the porch in an emotional standoff.

Wade broke the tension. "I'll keep her safe, Mr. Terrence. But it's important she takes a look at the scene to see if she can recall any details that may have been suppressed or missed."

"And you'll catch this creep who's been stalking our girl?" Aaliyah's mom interjected.

Wade exchanged looks with Aaliyah before responding. "That's my intention."

"Good." Her father's affirmation was directed at Wade, but his blue eyes drilled into Aaliyah's. "And we do need to talk."

"I know," she acquiesced quietly. But her parents needed to realize that she was hurt. Her trust in them was broken. Questions dangled everywhere, and she couldn't even cast her attention on them because, at the moment, she was trying to stay unharmed and alive.

Her dad moved to the side, seeming to give in to the fact that Aaliyah had no intention to take part in a conversation of the heart and soul in this moment. She mustered the willpower to continue to avoid her mom's gaze. One look at the woman who had loved her, nurtured her and cherished her and Aaliyah knew her resolve would melt. She loved her adoptive mom. Her dad too. It was just terribly hard to reconcile what she'd experienced and believed growing up with the new truths now come to light.

Aaliyah paused as she moved to walk past her dad. She met his gaze, and for a moment, they didn't say anything. Then she turned to Wade.

"I'll be back in a bit. Let me get the packs, and then we can head out."

Wade nodded and leaned against the porch rail.

Aaliyah had prayed that Wade's presence on the porch would deter her parents from following her into the house. She hoped their innate sense of hospitality would guilt them into staying to make small talk with the detective and leave Aaliyah to gather the supplies.

The Lord really did have a funny sense of humor. In a way, Aaliyah felt stalked from all sides. The killer on one, her parents on the other, Buck's suffocating protectiveness and Wade's constant presence—though she sort of was okay with that part.

Her prayer for solitude must have come just short of on time. As she hurried into the house after her go-packs, she heard her parents follow her inside. Aaliyah had a strong inclination that their attempts at confronting the situation were far from over.

Wade expected it, but when it happened, he still wasn't entirely prepared. Aaliyah charged from the house, two day packs thrown over her shoulder with metal water bottles secured on the sides. Tears streaked down her face, marring the otherwise porcelain skin dotted with freckles.

"Hey—" Wade reached for her on instinct, but Aaliyah rushed by him, Peaches on her heels.

"Aaliyah!" Mr. Terrence—Aaliyah's father—shouted after her, concern riddling his tone. He pushed his way onto the porch, Aaliyah's mom hovering in the background holding a tissue to her nose, her eyes red-rimmed. "Aaliyah!" Mr. Terrence shouted again.

Aaliyah ignored him as she hauled the packs from her shoulder and threw them in the back of the truck. Only she didn't climb into the truck as Wade expected. Instead, she marched into the woods just behind, pushing her way through the trees.

"Aaliyah!" The last shout from Mr. Terrence was accompanied by movement as he barreled down the porch steps to chase after his daughter.

Wade launched forward and grabbed his arm. "Sir!" His sharp, authoritative tone caused the older man to stumble to a halt. Mr. Terrence turned anxious eyes onto him. Wade had worked with desperate family members far too many times in the past. This was easier. This time, their daughter was merely estranged, not dead. "Sir, you need to give her space. Like she's requested."

"But—"

Wade had the immediate sense that Mr. Terrence was like a bull in a glassware shop. He barreled forward emotionally, without thinking of the further damage his actions could cause.

"Let me go after Aaliyah." Wade gave the man a solid pat on the shoulder.

"We just want her to understand why we did what we did," Mr. Terrence pleaded with Wade. "We didn't mean to betray her trust. Just—we wanted to protect her."

"From whom?" Wade narrowed his eyes.

"From the truth." Mr. Terrence responded without defensiveness. "From the fact she'd been tossed behind a church to die. Abandoned by her birth mother—or whoever—and left for the elements. How do you tell your child as they grow up that they weren't given for adoption out of love and concern for their welfare, but they were literally tossed into an alley?"

Wade couldn't answer. He wanted to. He wanted to explore even further. Had Aaliyah's adoptive parents ever crossed paths with Deborah Platt? Was there even more to the story that might still be hidden that could shed light on her case and, in turn, the recent cases of the victims Aaliyah and Peaches stumbled on?

But Aaliyah's form was fast disappearing into the hillside trees and brush, and Wade wasn't in the mindset to let her go off on her own, even on her parents' private property.

At this point, he frankly didn't want Aaliyah out of his sight. There was more than just her physical welfare at stake. There was her emotional welfare. And regardless of common sense, Wade knew that Aaliyah Terrence was becoming increasingly important to him with every ticking minute. He had no intention of letting the Arrowhead Killer get to her again.

Wade jogged after Aaliyah, hopping over rocks and maneuvering around serviceberry shrubs as he yelled after her. "Hold up!"

She waved him off, her yellow shirt a beacon as she charged further into the trees.

"Aaliyah!" Wade hadn't intended for his voice to sound as sharp and commanding as it did, but it served its purpose. Aaliyah stumbled to a halt and leaned back against the trunk of a pine tree.

Her chest heaved with barely suppressed emotion.

Peaches leaned against her legs, the dog's brown eyes pools of empathy, her muzzle nosing into Aaliyah's hand.

"Don't ask if I'm all right." Aaliyah stole the words from Wade's mouth as he pulled up to a halt a distance away from her so she didn't feel emotionally threatened by his presence. She leveled watery eyes on him, her chin quivering and her lips pressed together in an attempt to hold back emotion. "They said they were sorry."

Her hoarse, tear-filled words stunned Wade into a momentary silence. Saying apologies was a tiny first step toward healing, but it was a step, wasn't it? He wasn't a family counselor, he was a cold case detective. For the first time in a while, Wade was totally at a loss of what to do.

"They said they were sorry," Aaliyah repeated.

Wade calculated his response. He would give anything for a chance to return to the night before his sister had been killed. To be able to tell her he was sorry, to bust down the wall between them and to spare himself a lifetime of wishing things had been different. That he'd told Amy he loved her. That she was the best sister in the world. All the silly, cliché things people told siblings on greeting cards were all the things that no longer seemed silly to Wade. They were the important things that family too often failed to say.

Aaliyah wiped tears from her cheeks. "I want to just accept it." She leveled a desperate look on Wade. Her hazel eyes seemed to plead with him to help her process the emotions tangled inside of her. "I want to go back to last week, to when Mom and Dad were just that—my parents who loved me and raised me and were there for me, even now, as an adult. But sorry doesn't feel like enough."

There it was. The truth of it. The words so often fell short.

Wade dared a step closer to Aaliyah, now that it appeared she had no intention to escape. "Listen," he began, "I get that trust has been broken. That—" He tried to gather his thoughts and turn them into words. "But sometimes we also have to take into consideration the intent behind the actions taken. Sometimes the intent doesn't eliminate the wrong, but it helps us understand the why."

Aaliyah blinked at him, considering his words. Her hand moved to push away wayward red curls that bounced near her eyes. "What is their why? I understand when I was little, but now? As an adult, why hide the circumstances of my adoption? I'm not that fragile. I can take the fact someone threw me away."

"Would you have believed that your parents adopted you out of love, then, or would you question their reasoning and wonder if they'd taken you out of obligation?"

"Obligation?" Aaliyah frowned. She rubbed Peaches's ears, and the dog licked at her hand.

"Sure." Wade took a few more steps closer, bridging that gap that left him feeling like she was so far away from him. "An abandoned baby needed a home. Without one, you'd have gone into permanent foster care. You were left as a newborn to very possibly die. Would you believe they made you their daughter because they wanted a daughter, if they'd told you those circumstances? You wouldn't think that maybe they'd taken you because someone had to? That you were an obligation?"

Wade watched as Aaliyah considered his words. Her eyes darkened. She shook her head. "No. No because they love me."

"Right." Wade stepped even closer. Something about this woman awakened that gut instinct not just to protect but also to cherish. There was a tiny hollow of struggle in her eyes that told him she'd always felt abandoned, left behind, and probably even tried to believe she was truly wanted. That was the belief her parents had tried to spare her from, that belief that she was someone's burden to be cared for. Getting Aaliyah to believe that she wasn't a burden now that he'd come to town and revealed the truth around her birth? Wade owned that responsibility. He couldn't forsake the calling that he felt God had given him to help bring closure and healing to families broken by crime and violence. He did not want to be a part of wounding families further by being the harbinger of untold truths as he had been for Aaliyah.

"Please." Wade lifted his hand and allowed it to hover just above Aaliyah's cheek. Her liquid eyes pulled at him with need and hurt and a longing Wade couldn't define it, but it was there nonetheless. "Believe me, Aaliyah, I can see with my own eyes how much your parents love you. How their intentions—however wrongly they were enacted—were only to safeguard your heart."

He hesitated before allowing his fingertips to touch her skin. Her cheek was soft beneath his hand. Aaliyah's eyes slid closed.

Wade leaned in, feeling the magnetic pull and unable to resist it.

"Sometimes 'I'm sorry' really is the full encapsulation of regret," he whispered.

His words were a whisper-kiss of breath just above her lips. Aaliyah could feel Wade Marlowe, in a way she hadn't felt him since this entire horror story had begun. She could sense his strength exuding from his muscled body, she could hear the truth in his words that penetrated the hurt that had slowly been overtaking her heart and she could taste the expectation in his breath.

Circumstances were shoving them together, taking them places so quickly she could hardly put on brakes if she wanted to. Even Peaches seemed at ease, nosing her way between them, her muzzle pushing against Wade's leg while her tail thumped against Aaliyah's.

Wade's fingers trailed down her cheek and along her jawline. She had yet to open her eyes, but she could tell he was a mere inch away from his lips pressing against hers in a kiss. The type of kiss that reassured her she was still her own person, but he was standing by her, guarding, offering strength to her as needed and willing to go to battle on her behalf.

And he was right. She was angry that her parents had withheld the truth, but she was also battling those unanswered insecurities. Had she truly been wanted or had she been an obligation?

"Wade, I—" She opened her eyes. That was a mistake. Any willpower she'd had up to this moment to hold the man at arm's length dissipated in the chocolate depths of his eyes.

As they drew together, a low rumble growled in Peaches's throat.

Wade stiffened.

Aaliyah pulled back, awareness sparking through her and bringing reality coursing back.

Wade lifted a finger to the lips that had almost been pressed to hers. She nodded, recognizing the need for silence.

Another low growl from Peaches and she stood at attention, her black hackles rising on her neck and down her back.

Wade shifted in the direction Peaches was eyeing. The ponderosa pines grew tall, and then farther up the hillside, they grew thicker. Bitter cherry mingled with other shrubbery, making it difficult to see what Peaches had spotted.

Aaliyah narrowed her eyes. She listened for signs of wildlife that may have caught Peaches's attention. Doubtful a grizzly would be this close to them without having been startled. A mountain lion might lurk, but often they hunted from the trees, jumping onto the backs of their prey versus slinking through the undergrowth.

Peaches lurched forward, charging into the bushes.

"Peaches!" Aaliyah shouted. She knew better than to wildly chase after the dog. "I left the bear spray in the truck." A foolish move, and she of all people should know that. Bear spray was an excellent self-defense for more than just a bear raging at her because she'd startled it or gotten between it and some cubs.

Wade had pulled his sidearm, but he backed away rather than pursue. "Head back to the house," he stated, aiming his gun in the direction Peaches had run.

The dog was still barking, but Aaliyah couldn't tell by the tone of the barks if the dog sensed danger or was on the trail of another animal and inspired by instinct. It was apparent the dog was on the move by the sound of her barks.

"She's by the creek," Aaliyah offered, even as she listened to Wade, and they backed out of the area.

"Do you see bear or lion around here often?" Wade swept the area side to side.

"Occasionally. More in the evening or early morning." Aaliyah knew in her gut this was not a bear or a wildcat. It wasn't a coyote or a wolf. It wasn't even a stray dog or a feral tomcat. "Was it him?" she asked as they reentered the main yard, patchy with gravel and thin areas of grass.

Wade holstered his gun, but he met Aaliyah's eyes with a dark look of concern. "I don't know."

"Do you think the killer is following us?" Aaliyah glanced toward the house. Her parents had abandoned the porch, and for now, all was quiet. Peaches's barks had subsided. "I need to get my dog." She took a step back toward the tree line.

"Call for her but stay here." Wade's hand on her arm stopped her.

Aaliyah knew he was right. She called for Peaches, raising her voice to be heard and praying the silence from the black Lab was nothing to be worried about.

A few thick seconds passed, and then Peaches bounded into view. Her body language had shifted from defensive and back to her happy smile, pink tongue hanging from the side of her mouth as she jogged toward Aaliyah.

"Hey, girl, what was it?" Aaliyah squatted to greet Peaches. The dog trotted past Wade, who was still scanning the area. "What'd you see, girl?" She rubbed the sides of Peaches's neck, her hands roving the dog to be sure there were no injuries.

"I don't see anything," Wade determined.

Aaliyah would have answered, but she couldn't. Her fingers had grabbed hold of a thin cord hooked around Peaches's collar. It was the circumference of a bracelet, and to Aaliyah's horror, as she unclipped it, an arrowhead charm slid into the palm of her hand.

"Wade." Even she could hear the ominous tone in her voice as she said his name. "He was here. He left his calling card."

The cheap, dime-store arrowhead bracelet, so much like the others that had been left on his victims and in the front seat of her truck, dangled from Aaliyah's fingers.

The Arrowhead Killer wanted her to know he was close by. He was watching. And he could get close to her—Aaliyah curled her fingers into Peaches's fur—even to the ones who loved her the most.

NINE

The drive into the Bob was a good forty-five minutes of bouncing along rutted, gravel roads. The deep valleys created significant drop-offs with guardrails nonexistent except in the most tenuous of places. By the time they'd reached the narrow, one-lane dirt path that would take them deeper and nearer to the burial grounds, Aaliyah was itching to get out and hike. Wade pulled off the road as it reached an impassable end. They both exited, Peaches hopping out and wagging her rear end in anticipation of the wilderness hike. Wade retrieved their packs, and Aaliyah swung hers onto her back, removing the bear spray and hooking it to her belt to make it more accessible should it be needed. It was more likely to run into a bear now, at the higher elevation, and while they didn't scare her, she had a healthy respect for them.

"The investigation has cleared out of the area for now," Wade informed her. They started off on a trail, grass brushing against their legs. "Buck said it's a waiting game for the other four victims' bodies to be identified."

"There are over one million acres in the Bob Marshall Wilderness," Aaliyah said as they hiked. "Why choose an area to bury his victims where it was mostly accessible by vehicle and more easily discovered? I mean, I get he'd still need to carry the victims from the pull-off, but there are even more remote places that would be less likely to be discovered."

Peaches trotted ahead of them, her nose to the ground in relaxed curiosity. Wade's jaw flexed as he considered Aaliyah's question. "Accessibility, probably. It's not practical to pack a body in, even with a pack mule. He'd want to be rid of the victims sooner rather than later, and he certainly wouldn't want to be seen with them."

"Do you think he maybe *wanted* someone to find them one day?" Aaliyah couldn't help but entertain the idea that the Arrowhead Killer was feeding off the recent attention.

Wade tipped his head back and forth as if weighing his answer. "Like Eric said, there's no evidence that he's in it for the show. I'm wondering if there's not a loyalty in him to Deborah, to the arrowhead bracelets—to you. I'd suggest he wanted his victims in an area he could get to more easily than on horseback. I think…" Wade let his words hang.

Aaliyah toyed with the GPS she held. She was uneasy at the way Wade avoided finishing his thought. "You think what?" she pressed. She needed him to be honest with her.

Wade cleared his throat, his eyes fixed on the narrow gravel road ahead of him. "I think what Eric profiled makes sense. He's laid claim to Deborah. He's built a—a *story* around her, and now around you." The conclusion wasn't what Aaliyah had expected.

"How so?" She sidestepped a dried pile of elk scat on the ground.

"When I chatted with Eric again last night, he'd run the details of the case by another profiler friend of his who works for the FBI. Now, don't get too creeped out by this—but it was theorized that maybe our killer imagined Deborah and her pregnancy was his family of sorts. When things didn't go right, he killed her. You'd already disappeared and were lost to him. From then on, the other victims were attempts to recapture that story he'd dreamed of. He's not a killer for the random thrill of it. He killed the other three women out of frustration that they weren't Deborah. Now that you've resurfaced, both by finding the graves and somehow becoming clued in to the fact you're Deborah's daughter, that dream has become a true possibility again."

"But he tried to kill me—not recreate something with me." Her argument had merit, and even Aaliyah knew that.

"Maybe he didn't know who you were at the beginning. Now that he does—maybe that's why he hasn't attacked again." Wade's shrug told Aaliyah he was theorizing on his own now. "I'm not a profiler, but I've worked on enough cases to see some trends. Consider the fact he marks his victims with the arrowhead bracelet. He, himself, has an arrowhead bracelet. He *likes* to be connected to his victims. He has a personal attachment through a tangible item, but, if the theory that Deborah was his first victim is correct, then *you* are now more tangible than anything or anyone else. You're the connector, and I don't think he quite knows what to do with that."

A coldness settled over Aaliyah as a thought came to mind that she was surprised she hadn't considered before and was wishing she hadn't thought of now. "Do you think—" she began, hesitated, then at Wade's quick glance, finished, "do you think he could be my birth father?"

The tightening of Wade's mouth as he pressed his lips together told Aaliyah what she needed to know. "I might be the daughter of a serial killer." The words ripped through her with the real possibility of their truth. "You'd already considered that, hadn't you?"

Wade looped his hands around the shoulder straps of his

pack. "It's been discussed, yes. But he could just as easily *not* be your birth father. He is likely a delusional man who functions well enough in society for no one to be the wiser. It doesn't mean he fathered you. It just means he may have included you, as an infant, in part of his grandiose ideas as to how Deborah would fit into his world. When she didn't cooperate, or when something—whatever it was—went south, he killed her."

"Maybe it was me." Aaliyah ventured softly, and she wasn't surprised by Wade's frown. She hurried to explain. "What if Deborah gave birth to me, and she really was the one who left me behind the church? When the Arrowhead Killer realized Deborah had gotten rid of me—" she swallowed at the loathsome idea "—then it tipped him over the edge of sanity. Without the baby, he and Deborah and— and I—couldn't be a family."

Wade's silence told Aaliyah he was considering her theory and that he must not have considered that Aaliyah disappearing from the killer's radar as a baby might have been the final push to set things into motion. He cleared his throat. "I think a more pressing question, for now anyway, is *how long* has he known you're Deborah's biological daughter?"

"At least since he called me that night in the park."

"Right." Wade stepped over a fallen sapling. "But his behavior changed after the first day. Before he ever called you."

"I don't follow what you're saying." Aaliyah frowned.

Wade reformed his explanation. "When you stumbled on the graves and when he chased us later, he had no hesitation in trying to kill you. But then, something changed between then and when he was in your house—and when he abducted you. He made zero effort to end you. There were mere hours between when he grazed my arm and when he attacked us in your house. To go from trying to kill to not killing when he obviously could have? There's no way that could just be a coincidence."

Aaliyah noted the grove of trees in the distance where Peaches had originally found the skull. Yellow tape still cordoned off the area, which clearly had been tamped down by the investigation. "So what are you saying?"

Wade veered toward the burial site.

"I'm saying he went from trying to kill you to hesitating and leaving you alive. When he abducted you, and he left you tied up. He didn't even really hurt you aside from making you lose consciousness in a rather gentle way."

"Strangulation?" Aaliyah's voice went up an octave in disbelief.

Wade offered a sheepish laugh. "Well, as weird as it sounds, yes. He could have knocked you out like he did at the graves. He could have caused a severe concussion. He could have *killed* you. So why didn't he? What changed in twenty-four hours?"

"He grew a conscience?" Aaliyah's attempt at weak humor earned her a half smile from Wade.

"No." Wade hefted a deep breath.

"He's part of the investigation," Wade repeated. "Or he overheard something somewhere between those of us who knew. However it happened, he's closer than we've given him credit for. I don't believe, if you saw him face-to-face, you'd be looking into the eyes of a stranger."

"Wade?" Aaliyah heard the shaking quiver in her voice.

Wade's eyes darkened with honesty. "I believe if you met him right now, you'd be looking into the eyes of a friend."

Buck.

The name hung unspoken between them.

* * *

Wade watched Aaliyah as she hiked around the burial grounds. They'd already been combed over by the forensics team, but he could see the concentration on Aaliyah's face. She wanted to find something new. She wanted explanations not just for the murders—for her birth mother's murder—but for the personal attacks on her. Most of all, Wade knew she was desperate to uncover something that would point them away from people she knew and toward a stranger. A suspect to whom she had no emotional connection. Wade had a feeling if the culprit turned out to be anyone from Park Springs—namely, if Buck was in any way involved—Aaliyah would be heartbroken. This place was her home, her sanctuary, and the folks that surrounded her were literally her rescuers. She had been grafted into a home and a community that—whether they'd been aware of Aaliyah's abandonment as an infant or not—had embraced her and made her their own. Now she protected their vast wilderness. She helped manage their wildlife, the campers and outsiders who visited the area, and she reinvested herself into the land and its people.

This was a new side to cold case investigations that Wade hadn't bargained for. He'd had a reckless imagination that made him believe there was heroism in closing a cold case. That there was finality for families in identifying unknown victims and concluding who their killers were. But he'd been wrong. Instead, he was kicking a hornet's nest, and now the very person he was trying to protect was getting stung—repeatedly.

Aaliyah pointed toward the hillside. "A few years ago, we had wildfire over that ridge."

Wade waited, assuming she had a reason in pointing that

out. She hiked forward, skirting the burial sites and moving away from them.

"Fire danger is low right now," she continued. "Gordon was working on the trail conditions report for this district a week or so ago. Lots of trails are open, but there are some blowdown conditions." Aaliyah stepped over a fallen pine as if making her point. She looked over her shoulder at Wade to confirm he was listening to her. "We've recommended anyone traveling with stock to bring tools in case a trail needs to be cleared. We try to keep up, but there are miles and miles of trail."

Wade frowned, pausing as Aaliyah stopped and surveyed the land before them. Pine dotted the hills; the sky covered them in a blanket of blue. The ridgeline had patches of snow even though it was June.

"The rivers are high from melt right now too," Aaliyah finished.

"Aaliyah," Wade began. He had to bring her back to the present. He could sense she was closing off. Drifting away to the place she was most comfortable—the wilderness—and away from the stark reality they were currently in.

She turned toward him, her brows drawn together, her hazel eyes startling with the intensity of her thought. "Do you know approximately when the bodies were buried here? We could match them with the environmental records. That might also help explain why the killer buried them here. It might tell us a little bit about him as well. Is he well experienced in the Bob? If there were impending wildfires at the time of a burial, had he mapped out this area as typically outside a risk zone? Because a lot of campers who come to the Bob from out East don't think to look at those influences on the area. They just think, 'Ooh, nice spot to camp and fish.' But this place is wild. It's not always that simple."

Wade could see her line of reasoning now. Once the victims recently uncovered here were dated, they'd know better the ecological impacts around the time of their deaths. Were they killed here? Were they simply buried here? What could forensics show in their remains that might lend clues as to who the killer was?

They were all good and valid thoughts, but unlike on the television shows, those types of results took time. It wasn't a twenty-four-hour turnaround, and they could be talking months before learning the victims' identities—if they could be identified—what their cause of death was and the approximate time frame of their murders.

In short, they were back to trying to sort out the killer based on what they knew from his first victim, Deborah Platt, and from what Aaliyah had experienced and witnessed in the last week.

"Does anything here trigger any other memories from the day Peaches found the graves?" Wade attempted to bring Aaliyah back to what they could potentially achieve today.

Aaliyah shook her head. Her copper curls glistened in the sunlight, tied back in a loose bun at the nape of her neck. She was, in so many ways, a wilderness princess. She looked at home here. Her shoulders had lowered as stress seemed to seep from her muscles, and even now, Wade saw her chest rise and fall in a silent but deep breath of fresh wilderness air. It was dry and crisp air, spiced with the scent of pine, of freshwater river just beyond them hidden in the knoll and of the wild grasses that tangled at their feet.

"I remember very clearly that day, Wade." Aaliyah turned and began to make her way the few steps back toward him. "I remember the skull." She gave a visible shiver. "Then I followed Peaches to the site." Aaliyah pointed at the burial grounds. "I saw the bracelet then was hit from behind. That's it. That's all I remember leading up to being knocked unconscious. When I came to, the bracelet was gone, the attacker was gone, and I called Gordon for aid."

"And you didn't recognize the bracelet? You'd never seen anyone you knew wearing it before?" Wade watched Aaliyah's reaction.

She winced. "You mean Buck?"

"I mean, anyone you know." Wade wasn't going to drop any accusations on Buck or anyone else. There were suspicions, that was all. But years ago, there had been suspicions on Charlie Beedle too. Suspicion didn't mean guilt.

Aaliyah shook her head. "No. It was too fancy for anyone I know to have worn it. It reminded me of something like an award, you know? Something you'd put on a shelf or keep as a memento and only bring it out from time to time."

"Like when you visit the bodies of your victims?" Wade offered.

Aaliyah shrugged.

Wade squelched any outward evidence of his disappointment. He had hoped coming here might jog something in Aaliyah's memory. Maybe she'd seen the attacker's arm, maybe he had a tattoo, or she'd noticed the brand of shoe he wore…anything.

For a moment, Aaliyah stared at him. He could tell she wanted to apologize, but he was glad she didn't. It wasn't her fault. None of this was her fault, and she shouldn't take one iota of responsibility for any of it.

"I guess let's head back to the truck." It was a half-mile walk to the road from the burial grounds. "We'll go back to Park Springs and…" Wade let his words hang. And what? What next?

Aaliyah managed a wobbly smile. "I guess I'm not much help."

Wade shook his head. "You've been through a lot this last week." He gentled his tone. It was hard not to want to step closer to her, to push that one wayward curl behind her ear, to trail his fingers down her cheek. "The fact you're even trying to help is brave."

Aaliyah took a step closer, surprising Wade. He could smell something sweet wafting from her. An apple scent, maybe from her shampoo? She lifted her eyes, her words bordering on breathy. "I feel braver when you're around."

The wilderness stilled between them then. Wade resisted—or tried to. He had known her such a short time. Circumstances had thrust them together. Trauma was not a good foundation for romance, and yet here she was, lifting her face to his. There was vulnerability there, but also strength. A pleasing mixture of the strength of a capable woman and the desire for a counterpart to protect her as well.

Wade threw resistance to the wind. He lifted his hand and pushed the curl behind her ear. He lowered his head, his eyes searching hers. "I'll be your backup any day, Aaliyah Terrence."

And then he pressed his mouth to hers. He didn't bother to test her desire with a featherlight kiss. No. Wade kissed her, taking her lips and hungrily caressing them with his. His hand wove into the knot of coppery silken hair at the back of her head. Peaches woofed somewhere to the right of them, but it held no tone of danger. Wade ignored the dog and deepened the kiss with the woman in his embrace. Aaliyah's arms snaked around his neck, and she pulled herself closer to him. She was not shy in her kiss, and her lips told him that he hadn't been the only one resisting the draw that kept tugging them together.

After a moment, Wade broke the kiss, pulling back just enough to create a small distance between them. He could taste her, sweet like strawberries, on his lips and tongue.

"I—" he started, but Aaliyah's finger rested on his mouth, shushing his words.

"I don't want to try to figure this out too," she whispered. "Let's be okay that it happened." There was a pleading in her eyes, in her voice, that told Wade she wanted something new she could trust, while all the old in her life seemed to be unraveling. That new was him.

Yes, she could trust him.

Aaliyah regretted it the moment she put her finger over Wade's lips and silenced him. Of course she needed to figure this out! This dynamic between them, so quickly forged, was growing. It was unexpected, and it split her nerves in ways she wasn't sure how to manage. A part of her was utterly terrified. She was still treading water through the waves of half-truths and secrets being revealed in her own life, and now she was allowing a stranger in where trust and security would be required? But the other part of her felt reckless. No. Not reckless. Needful. She needed Wade and the strength he seemed to offer in a way she had not anticipated. Was this God's way of showing her that trusting was always an act of faith?

She took off at a brisk pace, and Wade kept up with her, long strides matching hers as they returned to the truck. They'd been out here for a few hours now, and nothing— absolutely nothing—had triggered new memories for Aaliyah. Whistling, she made sure Peaches followed. The dog bounded out and ahead of them, seemingly aware they were returning to the vehicle.

Once there, Wade slid into the driver's seat, and Aaliyah climbed into the passenger side. Peaches hopped up and between them, perching proudly and looking out ahead of them on the road.

Silence reigned between them. Aaliyah stole a glance at Wade. He was concentrating on maneuvering the truck along the one-lane, narrow dirt road. If they met an on-coming vehicle, they'd have to find a pullout, or one ve-hicle would need to back up and find a wide enough space to pass by. There was nothing in Wade's quiet expression that revealed his thoughts to Aaliyah. Was the kiss just a kiss, or did he hope for more? Or was she overthinking? Yes. Probably. Overthinking was a bad habit of hers. Maybe she should follow her own advice. Maybe she shouldn't try to figure it out. She could let it work itself out organi-cally and—

"Woah." Wade pumped the brakes as they were on a downward slope. The ridge rose on Aaliyah's side with marginal room for a shoulder. It was a drop-off on Wade's side, with a significant canyon ensuring massive injury—if not death—were a vehicle to go over the side.

Aaliyah grew alert, stiffening as the truck felt like it was picking up speed instead of slowing to a controlled, downward drive.

"Something's not right—" Wade bit off his observation, a deep frown creasing between his eyes. He shifted into a lower gear in an attempt to slow the truck. Another pump of the brakes and Aaliyah's eyes widened.

"Did you lose brakes?" She gripped the door.

Wade tried again, his leg pumping up and down. "I got

nothin'." The brake pedal went to the floor with no resistance.

The truck was picking up speed in spite of the lower gear.

"Shift down!" Aaliyah urged him.

Wade followed her advice, going down another gear. The truck swayed, and he wrestled the steering wheel to maintain control. Even Peaches seemed to sense the impending danger, and she whined, lying down on the seat.

The bank flew by her window faster, the brush and grasses becoming blurry as the truck continued to barrel down the gravel road. A curve was ahead, and Wade's knuckles whitened as he gripped the wheel.

"Use the emergency brake!" Aaliyah cried, grabbing hold of Peaches's collar. She should have bought that harness that you could buckle your dog safely with.

"Not yet." Wade's teeth were clenched with intensity. "That could put us into a massive swerve, and we'll go right over the edge of that curve. Hang on."

Aaliyah sucked in her breath, holding Peaches with one hand and bracing herself on the dash with her other.

Wade grimaced as the truck bounced over washboards in the road, and the curve came at them like an obstacle determined to kill them. He wrestled the wheel, and Aaliyah squeezed her eyes shut, praying silently.

Please, God. Help us make the corner. Steer the truck around the corner.

If they didn't make it, the truck would go straight off the side and into an instant fall down the canyon. The truck swerved, its backend fishtailing as they careened around the corner. The side mirror on Aaliyah's door snapped off as it connected with a tree. Barely skirting the corner, Wade fought with the wheel.

"Hang on." His tone was grave, and he reached for the emergency brake. When it engaged, the truck flung wildly.

Peaches fell against Aaliyah, and she grabbed her dog.

Wade shouted, losing control of the vehicle.

Aaliyah saw the chasm of open air ahead of them and the deep cavern that awaited. On her side, the shoulder opened, but a mass of rock and boulders was no comfort for a soft end.

She sucked in her breath.

Wade's shout mingled with Aaliyah's scream, and she bent over Peaches, burying her face in the dog's neck just as she sensed the truck fly completely out of Wade's control.

TEN

Something wet lapped the side of her face. Aaliyah moaned, lifting her head where it leaned against the door frame. A whine alerted her, and she blinked several times, willing away the blurry vision. Peaches continued to lick her temple, and Aaliyah lifted her arm, running her hand along the dog's head.

"Peaches," she mumbled. "Are you okay, girl?" The dog nosed Aaliyah's neck with her black muzzle, as if to find reassurance that her mistress was alive. The truck was crunched, having collided with the boulders. Wade had somehow managed to steer it away from the drop-off, but the rock wall they had hit had deployed the airbags and shattered the windshield.

"Wade?" Aaliyah strained to see around Peaches and the debris as well as the white polyester from the airbags that had deflated, leaving behind a powdery residue and the distinct smell of burning rubber. "Wade?" Aaliyah tried again. She saw him leaning over the steering wheel, his arms at his sides, a cut on the side of his temple dripping blood onto the deployed airbag. "Wake up." Aaliyah swallowed the panic that clogged her throat as she struggled to unbuckle her seat belt. Graciously, Peaches sensed she was in the way, and she scurried out the broken front window.

Aaliyah's momentary concern of glass cutting the dog's paws was overwhelmed by the unresponsive form of Wade.

His eyes were closed. His breathing was steady but light. Aaliyah squirmed from the constrictive dash that had been shoved inward by the crash, thankfully not pinning or breaking her legs. Once free, she crawled onto the seat, grateful there wasn't a center console to contend with. Her knees pressing into the seat, she reached for Wade, her fingers pushing away some of his hair to reveal the wound that was bleeding. It wasn't a deep cut, thank God, but he was definitely not conscious. She felt his pulse. Steady and sure. He was more than likely concussed. Aaliyah assessed the rest of Wade's body. His legs beneath the steering wheel didn't appear to have any open wounds or breaks.

Peaches paced outside the truck, barking every few seconds. Aaliyah pulled away from Wade. She needed to get help.

She needed to get her sat phone. Remembering she had it in her day pack on the floor of the truck by her feet, Aaliyah repositioned so she could reach for the pack. It was stuck in the crumpled innards of the truck. She strained to get her hand into the side pocket where the sat phone was lodged. On feeling it, Aaliyah worked until she could tug it free. The state of the sat phone did not encourage her.

"That's not good," she muttered to herself. The phone was crushed, its screen completely shattered and the thick antenna broken. Aaliyah tried anyway, going by memory instead of the display on the phone. But there was no tone, no light, no power. With a cry, she tossed it into the back of the truck and slumped in the seat. Willing herself to remain calm, Aaliyah determined her next move.

"Peaches, come," Aaliyah commanded. The dog trotted around the truck to Aaliyah's side. She eyed her dog and prayed that Peaches would somehow understand. The dog might be the quickest and most effective source of help—but only if Peaches comprehended her mission.

Aaliyah met Peaches's liquid brown eyes. The dog knew the ranger station. She knew Gordon and the other rangers. That was the best route for help. "Go get Gordon," she said to the dog. Peaches tilted her head as if trying to understand. "Go to the station. Go get Gordon."

After the command, Peaches whined, prancing from foot to foot as if verifying with Aaliyah that she should indeed leave her mistress behind.

"Go." Aaliyah's voice cracked with emotion, and she swallowed to control it. "Get Gordon."

Peaches wheeled around with a bark, and Aaliyah gave an inward cheer as the dog took off down the road in the proper direction.

Aaliyah watched until Peaches was out of sight. Praying the dog really did understand what she'd asked of her, Aaliyah readjusted her position.

She had to get out of the truck and try to get help herself. They were miles from Park Springs. The ranger station would be the nearest place to head for help, but even that was a strenuous hike considering she ached in every joint of her body. The best she could hope for was another vehicle that might choose to traverse the road at dusk. The truck had crashed between campsite areas. Pack horses would more than likely already be well into the wilderness by this time of day, not pulling into the trail pull-offs to begin their ride.

Aaliyah collected her breath and managed to maintain her sense of place. She knew this area. A small portion of the Bob Marshall Wilderness, south of the looming majesty of Glacier National Park. The Flathead River would

run not terribly far from here, but hiking in on a trail in the
hope of coming across a camper would be a worse choice
than staying to the main road.

The next few minutes, Aaliyah focused on pulling herself from the truck. Windshield glass had shattered into a
marbled mess of debris. Once her feet found solid footing,
she limped in a circle around the truck. There was no evidence of fuel leaking or anything that might ignite. A fire
out here would be bad on multiple levels. She was not eager
to see a wildfire start along with everything else.

She tugged on the driver's side door, and it opened with
a metallic groan. Wade hadn't moved, and he still appeared
unconscious. Aaliyah debated on moving him from the
truck, or if it was better to leave him where he was. If he
had anything broken, immobility was preferred, however,
without knowing the full condition of the truck, she wasn't
particularly keen on leaving Wade behind, slumped over
the wheel. And then there were wild animals to contend
with. Calculating the approximate distance she may need
to hike before making it to the ranger's station, she knew
Wade could be exposed for hours before help came.

Aaliyah finally made her decision after further assessing Wade's form. She took the next several minutes to work
cautiously in making sure Wade was free from any en-
trapping metal from the truck. After unbuckling him, she
slowly encouraged his body away from the wheel, holding
his head and neck carefully as she leaned him backward.

"C'mon, Marlowe," she said under her breath, "a little
help would be nice."

There was no response to her wry admonition. Wade's
eyes remained closed even as Aaliyah helped his body lean
back on the driver's seat. With his frame more fully exposed, Aaliyah reexamined his legs, his feet, his hips and

his chest. There didn't appear to be any breaks, but she couldn't know for sure. Broken or cracked ribs were definitely a risk, and while his breathing remained steady, she prayed nothing had punctured a lung—or worse.

With Wade repositioned as comfortably and securely as she could make him, Aaliyah rummaged in the back seat for his day pack. Finding it, she was able to pull out his can of bear spray, and she set it within easy reach of him along with his metal water bottle in case he came to and needed either of them. She rechecked his pack, already knowing she'd been the only one with a sat phone. He had a first aid pack, some energy bars, a flashlight and some rope. Basic.

"Okay." Aaliyah pulled back from the truck and rested her hands on her hips. Hills and bluffs merged into distant mountainous regions; it was all beautiful, but vast and wild. "I stick to the road," she admonished herself. After collecting what she could from her pack and Wade's, she combined them into one, making sure she had a water bottle for herself, the GPS and her can of bear spray.

She looked toward the sky, assessing the position of the sun to the horizon. There was time yet before the sun fully set and before complete night set in. Dusk often seemed to arrive and then linger here, the broad skyline and the early summer contributing to the longer days.

With a last look toward Wade, Aaliyah started forward, her boots crunching on the dirt road. She hadn't even taken time to consider why the brakes had given out in the first place, but there was conviction in her gut as she trudged down the road that this had not merely been a happenstance accident.

Aaliyah reached for the bear spray clipped to her side. Reassured it was there, she glanced around her. If the Arrowhead Killer had followed them here, if he had cut the brake lines or something, then he could be just out of the way, watching.

Bear spray was good for defense against more than just a grizzly.

The motor in the distance alerted Aaliyah, and she stilled in her steps. Exhaustion was fast settling in but worry for Wade had kept her pressing forward for the past twenty minutes. Maybe Peaches had made it to the ranger station for help! Maybe this was merely a random person. Regardless, Aaliyah had no intention of allowing the vehicle to make it past her without flagging them down. And that wouldn't be difficult considering the breadth of the pass was still barely enough for two vehicles to pass each other side by side.

As she listened, she could identify the motor. Not a truck or even a camper, but instead, it sounded like an ATV. Aaliyah knew that there were limited trails and places where ATVs were allowed in the area. The Bob was applauded for being one of the most natural ecosystems across its miles and miles of wildland. Keeping off-road vehicles confined to specific areas was critical in continuing the preservation. But now, Aaliyah's heart skipped.

Gordon.

The ranger station had its own ATV, and if that was Gordon, there was a good chance Peaches had alerted him. It would have made more sense for Gordon to have gotten in his truck though, unless for some reason, he'd anticipated the potential need to go off the main road.

Aaliyah awaited the vehicle and whoever drove it. Another ranger besides Gordon would be equally as welcome. She caught a glimpse of a headlight and then the four large tires of the ATV.

Gordon!

He came further into view, expertly maneuvering around a pothole and washboards before pulling up in front of Aaliyah. The motor of the vehicle drowned out the beloved stillness of nature, but Aaliyah was half giddy when Gordon shut off the engine. Confusion spread across his face, creasing the corners of his eyes, which were so similar to Buck's. The brothers had been a pivotal part of Aaliyah's life, and she didn't even try to hide the tears that sprang to her eyes.

"Did Peaches find you?" They were the first words she could manage to get out through her throat choked with emotion. She envisioned Peaches safe and ensconced in the ranger station with fresh water and one of the dog bone treats Gordon kept stashed in the closet.

Gordon's perplexed look only deepened. He swung his leg over the seat of the ATV and stood, inspecting Aaliyah's face. "What happened to you?"

Aaliyah pointed haphazardly behind her. "Wade and I— the brakes went out on his truck, and we ended up crashing into a boulder."

Gordon whistled. "You're fortunate you didn't go over the embankment!" He leaned forward, eyeing her cheek. "You're all banged up."

Aaliyah nodded, urgency cresting inside of her. "And Wade is still back at the truck. He's unconscious. We need to get him help."

Concerned, Gordon turned and rummaged through his pack tied to the back of the ATV. "Let me clean up your face."

"No." Aaliyah's protest was met with a surprised look from her elder. Gordon frowned. She hurried to impress on him the critical nature of the situation. "We need to get back to Wade. We need to call in for medical assistance."

Gordon zipped his pack. He tipped his head to the ATV. "Get on behind me, then."

"Where's your sat phone?" Aaliyah asked as she climbed onto the vehicle, hugging her arms around Gordon's waist. His ranger shirt was damp from sweat, but she didn't care.

Gordon fired up the ATV.

"Gordon, where's your sat phone?" she repeated. They should call it in immediately and then go to help Wade.

Gordon didn't answer. The ATV jerked forward, spitting dirt and gravel from its rear tires. Aaliyah lurched against Gordon, holding tighter, her muscles growing stiff.

"Did you see Peaches?" she yelled above the noise.

Gordon must not have heard her. He took the road with ease, turning around curves with the subtly of someone familiar with them. Aaliyah tried to relax her muscles as they traveled back toward the truck. They would get to Wade, they would make the call for a medical evacuation, maybe Wade would have even regained consciousness.

The ATV bounced over the ruts in the road. Wind made Aaliyah's eyes water, and she ducked her head as tears formed.

"How much farther?" Gordon shouted.

Aaliyah lifted her head and tried to gather her bearings. "Not too much farther. Around that bend about a half mile up."

"Got it!" Gordon's response was firm. He was on a mission to get to Wade, and Aaliyah felt relief coursing through her. She never wanted to relive these events ever again. If this accident had been deliberate, Aaliyah wasn't sure she could keep helping with the investigation. As foggy as her mind was right now, she realized she was actually considering leaving Park Springs. She could pack up her truck, take Peaches and head farther west. Or maybe east. Go to the Midwest for a time, let things settle down and maybe figure out who she was after all of this.

The truck came into view even as the sun was dipping behind the range, making the earth a mixture of dusky grays and yellows, with the trees turning into deep green in the waning light. Aaliyah strained to look over Gordon's shoulder. Was Wade moving? Had he gotten out of the truck? Or was he still lying back against the seat where she'd left him?

"There it is!" she yelled loud enough for Gordon to hear.

He gave her a nod and pressed the throttle lever. The ATV gained speed, and Aaliyah held on tighter to Gordon. She appreciated his anxiousness, but it wasn't wise to speed up as they approached the wreck. They didn't know where Wade was exactly, and if he was disoriented and stepped out in front of them…

"Gordon!" Aaliyah hollered to get his attention.

The ranger made no effort to slow the ATV. As the accident site drew close, Aaliyah watched for Gordon to release the throttle.

Only he didn't.

They sped past the wrecked truck. Aaliyah caught a panicked look at the driver's seat, where Wade still slouched.

"Gordon, what are you doing!" she half screamed now.

He either ignored her or couldn't hear her. But Aaliyah knew something was dreadfully wrong. She twisted to look over her shoulder. The wreck was already out of view. Aaliyah pounded on Gordon's shoulder. "Stop! Where are you going?"

He didn't answer, but the speed at which he drove the machine kept Aaliyah from jumping off. She tried to read

Gordon's mind, tried to compose a logical reason why he would have sped past the truck and Wade's injured form.

She could only think of one, and it came to her as Gordon shifted, the collar on his shirt loose around the back of his neck. She'd never noticed before—never had a reason to—but a small arrowhead was tattooed at the base of his neck near his shoulder blades.

An arrowhead.

Everything in Aaliyah went cold.

He groaned. His head pounded like he was being hit repeatedly with a hammer. Wade blinked, struggling to open his eyes and get his bearings. When his eyes finally focused, he was quickly reminded of where he was. The brakes had gone out. He'd steered for the boulder, opting for rock over flying off the precipice.

Aaliyah!

Wade twisted in his seat, wincing and squinting as the world swam around him. She was gone. So was her dog. He lifted his hand to his temple, felt wetness and pulled his hand back to look at his fingers. Blood. He took a quick assessment of the rest of himself. Bangs and bruises. Nothing felt broken. Thank God, for that blessing! But where was Aaliyah?

He looked around him on the seat of the truck and noted his water bottle and a can of bear spray propped beside him. Aaliyah must have gone for help. She must have left these things near him in case he wasn't able to move on his own. Until help came.

Wade rested his throbbing head back on the headrest of the seat. How long had he been out? The sky was still lit, but it was darkening with the imminence of dusk. He heard the rumbling of a motor in the distance. Shifting, he managed to bully through the spinning that was activated by his movement. A lone headlight illuminated the inside of the ruined truck. An ATV barreled toward him, and Wade had an instant rush of relief. He could get help, he could make sure Aaliyah was all right, and then, he could find the underlying cause of why his brakes had gone out. He already had a suspicion.

The four-wheeler sped toward him. Wade kept his head laid back on the headrest of the truck in order to minimize movement and subsequent dizziness. He was able to make out a man on the front and what appeared to be a woman behind him. A woman with coppery-colored hair.

Aaliyah!

Excitement and relief coursed through Wade, but he frowned as the ATV came closer, traveling at a speed that showed no intent on stopping. Before he could push his body upright to flag the vehicle down, it sped past. Dust kicked up from behind its tires, leaving Wade and the ruined truck behind.

No!

Wade twisted in the seat to look behind him, ignoring the waves of pain that throbbed in his skull. Definitely Aaliyah. He could tell by her frame, by the hair, and she appeared to be attempting to look behind her. To look at him. He hadn't gotten a clear look at the driver. But whoever it was…

The thought hung in Wade's mind as adrenaline kicked in. There was no logic that could reason away any vehicle coming up on an accident site and blasting by it without concern. Not out here in the wilderness, anyway. Everything in Wade told him there was no way that if Aaliyah had any influence on the rescue, she would allow the driver to race by. Something was wrong, and though Wade's gut had already been churning with this premonition, the facts were the ominous exclamation point that emphasized it.

He shoved open the truck's door as best as he could. It was stiff on its hinges, bent and cockeyed. Wade managed to swing himself from the seat, resting his feet on the ground. Urgency soared through him, but his head made him fall against the door frame, dizzy.

"Get it together, Marlowe," he muttered to himself. He didn't have time to recuperate. Everything in him told Wade that whoever had been driving that ATV was not only behind the brakes going out on the truck, but also behind the recent events. If the driver wasn't the Arrowhead Killer himself, then he was somehow tied to him. A fact even more apparent was they were driving back in the direction of the killer's burial grounds. If they were headed there, it meant no good for Aaliyah.

Wade mastered his equilibrium and reached into the truck for the bear spray and his water bottle. He fumbled at his waist to locate his side arm. It was missing. Discomforted by that notion, he scrounged through the truck's remains as best as he could to try to locate it. To his chagrin, he saw it wedged and impossible to reach where the driver's side floor had crunched into a pancake with the front of the truck. He was blessed to be walking. Somehow, his legs had avoided being crushed, but the impact must have dislodged his gun and sent it flying.

"Okay. Think." Wade found it grounding to say his thoughts aloud. But they echoed in the vastness of the terrain. It would do no good to try to get help. He had noticed the remains of Aaliyah's SAT phone, and it was obvious that would be of no assistance. By the time he could hike to the nearest ranger outpost, odds were it'd be closed and locked for the day. By then, Aaliyah would likely be gone.

No. He had to follow the ATV. At the speed it was traveling, Wade would need to hike fast. The foreboding welling within him didn't help either. Everything told him he knew where Aaliyah was being taken.

The Arrowhead Killer's burial grounds.

ELEVEN

The moment the ATV slowed enough, Aaliyah flung herself from its back. She hit the ground, rolling away with stones and debris digging into her already bruised body. Gordon shouted, and the ATV jerked to a stop, spinning tires in the earth.

They were here. Back at the pull-off near the burial grounds. Aaliyah scrambled to her feet, her hands pawing at the ground and dirt clumping beneath her nails. She took a few stumbling steps before realizing her bear spray had come unclipped and fallen from the waistband of her jeans. Bear spray! Aaliyah spun back to find and retrieve it, but Gordon was charging toward her. She had no time to get the bear spray, and instead broke into a run away from her captor. At this point, she had no plan but to flee. To get away from Gordon—her partner and friend—before he turned into the monster she figured he must be.

"Aaliyah!" His voice reflected off her back. She ran harder, her lungs already exploding from the effort, her muscles screaming at her for pushing them further than they wished to go after the accident.

Aaliyah jerked backward as a meaty arm snaked around her waist halting her flight and flinging her against Gordon's chest.

"What are you doing?" he demanded as Aaliyah twisted and kicked and clawed at him.

Gordon's hold loosened and Aaliyah pushed off from him. "Leave me alone!" She whirled, her chest heaving, glaring daggers at the man she had trusted. The man she had worked with every day since she became a ranger. She swept an angry look over the man's face. It was almost expressionless. He didn't even look irritated that she had tried to flee. There was a curtain over his eyes that blocked her from being able to interpret his feelings. His emotions. If he even had any.

"It's been you, hasn't it?" Aaliyah accused. She had worked every day beside the man who had murdered Deborah Platt. The man who had taken her birth mother and left her body in the wilderness to decompose and be at the mercy of the animals. The man who had potentially been responsible for the other graves just beyond them and for her own recent assaults.

"Aaliyah." Gordon's voice was controlled. It was as if he were a lion tamer and was coaxing the wild in her to be still. "I need to show you something." He reached out a hand.

"I'm not going anywhere with you!" she spat.

Gordon waggled his fingers on his outstretched hand. "Please. Come. Let me show you."

"What? A new grave? Have you dug a fresh one for me?" Aaliyah didn't regret her mouthy retort. He deserved it. He deserved no respect and more.

There was a flicker in Gordon's eyes then, and Aaliyah noticed a muscle in his jaw twitch. "You're quite sure of yourself. Quite sure you understand."

Aaliyah eyed him, maintaining the cautious distance between her and her captor. "I know you're the Arrowhead Killer."

Gordon clicked his tongue. "Now, see, that is such a generic name. I would've thought they could have been more creative."

Aaliyah stared at him in disbelief. The man was truly ill in his mind if that was his largest concern. "You killed her. Deborah Platt. Didn't you?"

Gordon hefted an impatient breath and wagged his hand at her, palm up toward the sky. "Come. I need to show you something. I'd rather not force you, but then, so far, you've never given me much choice."

"You never gave *me* a choice." Aaliyah remembered being knocked senseless by him not so many days ago, right in this very region of the Bob. "You pistol-whipped me."

"I didn't know—"

"Don't tell me you didn't know it was me," Aaliyah interrupted, flipping a long loose curl of red hair over her shoulder.

"I wasn't going to. I was going to say I didn't know you were Deborah's daughter." Gordon's conclusion did nothing but solidify some of the assumptions she and Wade had made. "Now come."

Aaliyah took a tentative step toward Gordon. There was steel in his eyes that told her she dared not run again. He was faster, stronger, and as calm as he was, she had the distinct feeling he was very unstable.

"That's my girl." He smiled with encouragement and motioned for her to come with him. The burial grounds. He was most definitely taking her to the burial grounds.

Aaliyah hiked alongside Gordon, but she was anxiously trying to think her way out of his control. If she'd had her bear spray, she would have thought nothing of opening it up full force on Gordon, even though the concentrated pepper spray was enough to blind a man. But that was no longer an option. Physical prowess? She'd be overpowered in no time. Gordon was strong. He might have thirty-plus years on her, but the decades of working in this range kept him fit and muscular. She could run. She could hope to outrun him enough to hide. Doubtful she'd be successful.

She eyed his side. He had shot at her before, but now she didn't see a firearm on him, although that didn't mean he wasn't armed. Perhaps an ankle holster held a weapon. Aaliyah wouldn't put it past Gordon, but then he had his own can of bear spray at his side. He'd always told her he carried bear spray for the bears and major trouble, and a .22 to put down his horse if he had to. Other than that, a .22—and even various calibers of handguns—would do little against a raging grizzly. Bear spray held the power. Gordon held the only bear spray.

The grove of trees came into view. The yellow tape that had bordered the crime scene flapped in the wind, having been torn from its barricade. That had to have happened not long after she and Wade had vacated this area only a few hours before. When they'd gone, they'd left it undisturbed.

"Did you sabotage the truck's brakes?" Aaliyah wasn't in the mood for any sort of small talk, but a direct question with a direct answer would be nice.

Gordon shot her a sideways glance. "You really do think the worst of me, don't you?"

Aaliyah eyed him. "You mean you *didn't* tamper with the brakes?"

"I didn't say that." Gordon's evasiveness increased Aaliyah's irritation. She prayed that God would give her the opportunity to escape—that He would open a door of some sort where she could run and have the hope of getting away. On seeing the burial grounds, a dark and ominous foreboding was settling over Aaliyah. One that promised nothing good when Gordon was finished with her.

"What did you want me to see?" Aaliyah opted to play along. If she could get Gordon off guard, she'd at least have the element of surprise behind her.

"This." Gordon swept his arm wide, a grand gesture meant to include the disturbed burial grounds and the wilderness around them. "What do you see, Aaliyah?"

She had a keen sense there was something specific he wanted her to say, but reading his mind was impossible. She chose to answer with honesty. "I see a beautiful landscape marred by evil." Aaliyah dared to look Gordon directly in the eyes. "I see graves where living people should be camping, exploring the wilderness, living life. But instead, there are just graves. Places for the dead to rest, and now they can't even do that."

"No." Gordon's face darkened. "You disturbed their resting places. The authorities took them away, and now—now there is nothing." He crossed the invisible line where the yellow tape had once bordered the area. The long grass tangled with his khaki pant legs. He pointed to a grave, filled in now, but obviously having been disturbed and the remains removed. "That was a young woman from Kalispell. In fact," he glanced at Aaliyah, "she said she was originally from Minnesota. She had run away from home, and she was just passing through." Gordon squatted beside the grave, scooping up some of the loosened earth and letting it run through his fingers. "Just passing through. But that's not what they wanted."

Aaliyah took a step backward. Even a few feet of distance between her and Gordon could make a difference in an attempt to flee.

"What did they want?" She entertained Gordon's desire

to be heard. Wade had been right. Gordon was a story-teller, and after all these years, he wanted someone to listen to him tell it.

Gordon traced a name into the dirt with his index finger. *Mary.*

"They wanted a place to belong." That was his answer. It was poignant. It was, in another time and place, meaningful. Gordon had seen the wanderers as lonely people, and in truth, he was partly correct.

"So you killed them?" That was the piece of the puzzle Aaliyah could not reconcile.

"No, no." Gordon gave his head a short shake. "I rescued them. I helped them step into the light. I protected them. That is what family does, Aaliyah. They watch over, and they do whatever must be done to protect their loved ones."

"And that's what you did? Whatever must be done?" Aaliyah summarized, a bitter taste on her tongue at the idea that somehow Gordon seemed to think he was doing his victims a service.

Gordon stood, hands on his hips as he surveyed Aaliyah carefully. "Yes," he finally answered. "I give them their freedom. I watch them fly."

Wade's lungs burned as he half jogged up the road. If the killer had taken Aaliyah back to the burial grounds, then he'd have to go at least three miles on before arriving at the pull-off. Then there was the hike back to the graves. His head pounded, and each step was a labor of concentration. As he made his way, he tried to reason through the events of the day.

They'd been at Aaliyah's parents' ranch, and Peaches had run off only to return with that ominous bracelet tucked into her collar. Then they left in the truck and came here. Into the wilderness. Had the killer followed them? He would have to have been almost right behind them. He also would have needed to be comfortable with the terrain. Wade could only imagine someone unfamiliar with these roads would drive slowly and cautiously, but a local? To someone accustomed to coming here, like the killer, that would be a piece of cake. He could have easily followed them, parked a distance away so as not to be heard and then sabotaged the brakes on the truck. That meant, though, that after days of silence, the Arrowhead Killer had come to a conclusion—a plan—in regards to Aaliyah. And it didn't include keeping her alive.

Wade doubled over, gulping oxygen. It was an uphill jog, taxing for a fit person who hadn't just been in an accident and more than likely suffered a concussion. The road blurred in front of him, and he dropped to his knees.

"Lord, please." His prayer was no more than two words. God didn't need an explanation. He had seen all and been there through it all, but He certainly wouldn't allow the killer to win. He couldn't! Wade squeezed his eyes shut as a wave of pain shot nausea through him.

Not again. Not again! He had failed his sister, Amy, so many years ago. He would never forget their final words and the argument. If he had just gone after her, would he have changed the trajectory of her future? If he had just been with her—if only she hadn't been attacked so randomly. She was strong. He knew their argument had distracted Amy from being her normal, cautious self. If not for their argument, she would have been more aware of her surroundings, and she might still be alive. He had pledged to bring justice to the families of victims, but since meeting Aaliyah, he more than wanted to protect her. He *needed* to protect her. She was too precious, weaving her way too close to his heart, for Wade to ignore the responsibility.

Sure, maybe she hadn't asked him for his protection. She may not even feel the same. But after the kiss earlier, then the silence in the truck on the way down before the crash... Wade knew he could not lose her. Could not experience another person close to him being ripped away by the clutches of evil.

Wade retched on the ground, heaving as the pounding in his head sent spearing pain through the backs of his eyes.

God would need to grant him strength and an extraordinary amount of physical ability.

"I'm coming, Aaliyah," he whispered as he wiped his mouth with the back of his hand. Straightening, Wade allowed himself a few seconds to regain his stability, and then he started forward. "God, give me strength," he breathed.

Aaliyah eyed Gordon as he approached her. The pine trees around them swayed at the tops, and a bird fluttered from one to another, oblivious to the tension just below its wings. She glanced at his wrists. There was no arrowhead bracelet made of gold and silver. She'd never seen him wear a bracelet. Not even the simple black-corded ones like those left behind in her truck and on the victims.

"You came back for the bracelet that day, didn't you?" she accused.

Gordon didn't appear bothered by her accusation. "I don't wear it except on special occasions—like visiting the graves. Only it fell off my wrist, and so yes, I wasn't going to leave it behind. It's symbolic. I keep it safe at home most of the time when I'm not here."

"Why, Gordon?" It was such a basic question, but there were so many layers to the question of why. Aaliyah shrank away as Gordon stopped just in front of her, the graves behind him, mounds of abandoned earthen coffins.

Gordon's eyes snapped. "Why." It was a rhetorical state-ment. He acted as if the answer was so predetermined that it shouldn't even be a question. That it should just be known. He pushed his hand deep into the pocket of his trousers as he spoke, his reaction contemplative. "You know I always wanted a family?"

Aaliyah didn't want to answer honestly. The last two years of working in the station with him and their daily in-teraction here in the Bob had left plenty of time for them to chat about life. To Aaliyah, Gordon had always been a content, older bachelor—just like his brother, her godfather, Buck. He'd never once, that she could recall, mentioned a desire to be married or to have children.

"That perfect family of 1.5 children, a wife and a dog?" Gordon pulled his hand from his pocket. "That's always been what I wanted. Although," he lifted his eyes, "I pic-tured three kids."

There was something in his grasp, something small. Aa-liyah eyed it like it was a spider that might bite.

"We could still be that, Aaliyah—at least a portion of it." There was hope in Gordon's expression.

Aaliyah eyed him warily. "Be a family?"

"Yes." Gordon nodded emphatically. "I brought you here to show you the consequences of Deborah's decision to abandon you." He extended his arm toward the graves. "Just think! No one else would have died! Deborah wouldn't have died. It could have been the three of us. Together."

"I don't understand." Aaliyah's mind swam in confu-sion, trying to piece together the final parts of the puzzle. "You've never spoken of wanting a family."

"No. You've never shared your deepest dreams with me either." Gordon's retort hit its mark.

No. No, she hadn't.

"I had a girlfriend when I was in high school, back in the day, but that ended." He reached for Aaliyah's wrist with his free hand.

She jerked her arm back.

"Now, now." He claimed her wrist, and his grip pinched her skin. "I managed to get to my thirties without anyone seriously being interested in me. What was it about me a woman didn't want? I would have been so dedicated. There I was at thirty-seven years old, and I was already staring down middle age alone."

Aaliyah tugged on her wrist. This time Gordon yanked her forward, and his gray eyes hardened. "Stop. Fighting." He enunciated both words like a threat.

She listened. For now.

The sound of a hawk screeching in the sky above cut through the thickness that weighed between them. Gordon lifted the hand that clutched the item from his pocket. He let it dangle from his fingers. The thin, black cord with an arrowhead charm taunted Aaliyah.

With a whimper, she jerked against Gordon's grasp. She knew what that was. It was his tag, like someone tagged the ear of a mountain lion or a wolf. It told the world they were being watched and followed, and essentially, that they'd been taken.

"Then I met Deborah," Gordon continued, unaffected by Aaliyah's struggle to free herself. He slid the cord around her wrist and tightened the bracelet.

Aaliyah kicked at Gordon, and he sidestepped it, spinning her around so fast she felt her neck crack. His arm curved around her chest, pulling her back tight against him.

Don't say it. Please, don't say it. Aaliyah didn't want to hear the words come from Gordon's mouth. That he was her father. That he and Deborah had started the family he'd always wanted.

His grip crushed her, stealing her breath. Gordon pulled her backward with him. She dragged her heels, clawing at the branches for something to hold on to, clawing at his arm that held her in a vise-like grip.

Gordon's breath was hot in her ear. "She was going to have a baby. I was going to *be* there for her, when *he* wasn't. When the father had left Deborah to deal with it all by herself."

Aaliyah felt her body sag with relief. Gordon flung her to the ground, and Aaliyah spun as she fell, hitting the earth with her backside and scraping the heels of her hands.

Gordon wasn't her father!

The relief was palpable. Even though the danger was incredible, Aaliyah clung to the truth that Gordon could not lay claim to her as his own flesh and blood. She looked up at him from where she lay sprawled on the ground. The abandoned grave beside her was terrifying. It wasn't a gaping hole, having been filled in by the crime scene investigators, but it was still apparent what Gordon's long-term intent was for her.

"She told me the baby died." Gordon's voice went hoarse. He glared down at Aaliyah. "But you didn't die, did you?"

Aaliyah stared up at Gordon. "No. I'm very much alive."

"See?" His voice rose in hope again. "You can come back and—I'll take care of you. Like I was always going to."

"You've lost your mind." Aaliyah spat the words before she could think them through. "You just tried to kill me by taking out the brakes in the truck."

Gordon's face darkened. "I was trying to make a point— and get rid of Marlowe. You were—collateral damage. I figured Marlowe would steer away from the edge into the wall. And now, I'm giving you an opportunity, Aaliyah. This can all end with a future. It doesn't have to be like Deborah or—or the others. Just accept that I can take care of you. We can be the family we were meant to be."

She was dumbfounded. Did he really think that she would accept his reasoning—what little reason there was to it—and forget he'd committed murder?

"I have a family." The realization of her parents' love and care for her all these years was palpable. Their confrontation earlier that afternoon at the ranch was inconsequential now. So they hadn't shared the entire story with Aaliyah, but what did it change? She'd been concerned she was an obligation, and yet, hadn't the last twenty-five years of love and investment in her proven otherwise? "I have parents," Aaliyah stated as much for herself as for Gordon. She bit her tongue as she saw Gordon's expression. No. No, she needed to play along with him. Feed into his delusion. Rebellion would only wind up with her dead.

Gordon stared at her with assessment, and then he shook his head. "You're too much like Deborah. Too stubborn. Too willful."

Aaliyah struggled to sit up, stones digging into her palms as she pushed against the ground. "I'm sorry. I only meant that I have parents, but—I—I've never been wanted. And if—you want me, I—" Bile rose in her throat. She tried to struggle to her knees. "I'd like that." The lie made her ill.

Gordon eyed her for a long second and then wagged his finger and squatted beside her. He slipped a plastic band from his pocket and yanked Aaliyah's legs together at the ankles.

"What are you doing?" Aaliyah cried.

Gordon roughly handled the band around her ankles. "You're lying to me."

"No! No, I'm not!" She struggled against his hold, forcing him to sit on her legs. Aaliyah felt the band zip tight and dig into her skin.

"You're saying what you think I want to hear," he gritted, giving the tie one last skin-numbing tug.

"I'm telling you the truth! I've always been fond of you, Gordon!" And she had been. Gordon had been a constant in her daily life. But God was going to have to strike with lightning or something to change the course this day was on. She could see death in Gordon's eyes now. The intention of saving her to be his was gone, and now he had resigned himself to something far worse.

Gordon sucked in a deep breath, closing his eyes like he was meditating for a long moment. When he opened them, he seemed in control again.

"You know," Gordon began, irritatingly calm and unperturbed. "It never once crossed my mind Deborah's baby might have survived. That someone found you, adopted you—that you were right here, alive." He moved off Aaliyah's legs and shoved her to her side, grabbing her arms and zipping them in a second band behind her back.

Her arms throbbed. Aaliyah bit her lip to squelch a whimper. She didn't want to give Gordon the satisfaction of hearing the pain in her voice.

"Soooooo..." He drew out the word like a man thoroughly enjoying his power of narration. "There you were, under my nose for twenty-five years." Gordon observed Aaliyah as he rolled her forward and then helped her into a sitting position. He half dragged her a few feet and then let her lean back against the trunk of a pine tree. "And all of this could have been so much different. It could have been you and me, here in our wilderness—in the Bob—taking care of this place we love so much, as *family*." He towered over her form, staring down at her. "It's obvious you've made your decision in regard to that possibility."

Desperate, Aaliyah tried to convince him again. "No. No, I'd like that. I love it here, and you and I could be—"

"Stop." Gordon lifted a hand, disgust crossing his face. "You're a horrible liar."

They stared at each other for a moment, and Aaliyah accepted the fact she was not going to be able to play on Gordon's delusions. "What are you going to do now?" Aaliyah asked. She should keep him occupied. At least until she figured out how to get free. She'd not fought hard enough at the beginning. She should have taken the risk and made another run for it. Instead, she'd allowed Gordon to subdue her, and now there was not much she could do to escape.

Gordon approached the grave that had been filled in. He stood over it, hands on his hips, lips thinned in thought. Then he addressed Aaliyah with a quizzical look. "Were you happy?"

"I don't know what you mean." Genuinely confused, Aaliyah swallowed another surge of fear.

Gordon stared down at her. "With your adopted parents. Were you happy?"

"Y-yes," Aaliyah stammered. She would give anything to see her parents again. Their deception regarding her adoption seemed so minor now in comparison to Gordon's betrayal.

"Huh." Gordon kicked a stone as if her answer wasn't what he'd wanted to hear. He returned to her and squatted down, folding his hands together and studying her. "I would've been a good father to you. Deborah should have known that. I told her plainly I would take care of her and you. That she didn't need to keep drifting, to run away from Park Springs just because your father broke her heart and abandoned her when she got pregnant."

"Who broke her heart?" Aaliyah grasped Gordon's reference.

Gordon's brows furrowed a moment and then straightened. "The man who got Deborah pregnant."

"My birth father." In all of this, Aaliyah had barely considered her birth father, aside from hoping he wasn't also the Arrowhead Killer. "Who was my birth father?" she breathed.

"It doesn't matter," Gordon retorted. "Whoever he was, he abandoned Deborah. He abandoned *you. I'm* the one you should want to know. I'm the one who would have cared for you."

"If you're so caring," Aaliyah dared to ask, to challenge Gordon, "why kill more women after Deborah? What about the others?" She shouldn't have asked. Aaliyah didn't really want to know why Gordon had devolved after Deborah's murder. It was apparent he reveled in the control he exerted, and perhaps not having Deborah in his life had triggered that need to control someone else.

Gordon picked a long blade of green grass and dragged it between his thumb and index finger. "The others?" he repeated. "They were just there, needing somewhere to belong. And I didn't want to be alone. But they were so… disappointing, so I set them free."

She'd been right. Aaliyah had never wanted to be wrong so much in her entire life.

"I never should have killed her. I never *would* have killed her had I known you were alive." He lifted his eyes and shook the blade of grass at her, a sad smile quirking his lips. "It's crushing, Aaliyah. *You're* crushing me. I always enjoyed working with you here in the Bob. We share the same passions for the wilderness, for wildlife. We could have been a family, but Deborah had to tell me you died in childbirth. And then—what choice did I have? She was worthless to me without you. And now I have you, and you—want nothing to do with me." Gordon's final sentence ended, and an eerie, thick silence filled the air.

Aaliyah swallowed a lump in her throat. Why had Deborah said that? Had she abandoned Aaliyah not because she didn't want her but because she'd somehow seen through Gordon and sensed the danger? Had Deborah seen what Aaliyah never had up to this point with Gordon? That he was obsessive and *possessive*? That he would have built his world around Deborah and Aaliyah and slowly suffocated them beneath his control?

A movement in the trees behind Gordon caught Aaliyah's eye. She tried not to stare and draw attention to it.

Gordon leaned back on his heels. "That day you found this place?" He stuck the blade of grass in his mouth. "I knew you'd come out to check on campers, but I didn't know you'd come this far." He reached out and flicked the cheap arrowhead bracelet he'd tied around Aaliyah's wrist. "Mine is nicer of course," Gordon stated baldly. "And there you were. I didn't want you mixed up in this, Aaliyah. Before I even knew you were Deborah's kid and I started to hope things could be different, I wouldn't have wanted you caught up in this drama."

His need to reassure her distracted Aaliyah from following the flash of blue in the trees. Someone was circling them. Someone was watching!

Aaliyah cleared her throat to make a noise so Gordon would continue to focus on her. If that was a camper, they were not only a potential rescuer, but they were also in danger. If it was a fellow ranger or even a trail guide—maybe Peaches *had* succeeded in finding and retrieving help.

"How did you find out?" Aaliyah asked the question not only because she needed to know, but also to retain Gordon's attention.

His graying brows raised. "Find out? That you were Deborah's baby?"

Aaliyah nodded.

Gordon's chest hefted in a large sigh. He pushed off his thighs into a standing position. "Sheer coincidence. I went into the station that evening after I took shots at you and that detective boyfriend of yours." A shadow crossed his face and he winced. "I didn't want to kill you, Aaliyah. You've been my partner and—I didn't want to, but I was afraid you'd seen me. Could identify me."

"I hadn't seen you." Aaliyah delivered her words in monotone. Another flash of movement caught her attention.

"Well, I didn't know. I went to the station—I do that often to stop in and see Buck. I overheard him and that Wade Marlowe talking about why Marlowe was in town. DNA, he said. Claimed he'd identified not only the unknown woman from years ago, but also her daughter. They'd obviously talked before on the phone. Buck said your name. Your detective friend affirmed it, and then I knew. You. You, Aaliyah, were Deborah's baby girl."

Aaliyah's eyes filled with tears. Not just from the emotion of the unveiling of her own history, but because of the series of events that had brought them here. To this place in the Bob. To the base of a pine tree, and an empty grave, an arrowhead bracelet, and Wade...

She saw Wade, circling from behind.

Somehow, he had found them.

TWELVE

Wade crouched behind a small spruce, its thick branches hiding him from Gordon, whose back was also turned to him. He'd managed to make it to the burial ground, and now his anger boiled at a slowly rising temperature. Gordon? Gordon Halstead, the sheriff's brother? *Buck's* brother?

So many questions riddled Wade's mind. How had Buck not seen this in his brother? Why did Gordon have such an investment in Aaliyah? But now wasn't the time for questions, even though he heard Aaliyah posing some of the same ones he wanted to.

Wade knew Aaliyah had spotted him. There had been a brief flicker of awareness that crossed her face, but now, all credit to her, she was hiding her recognition of him well. Thankful for the gift of adrenaline, Wade ignored his throbbing head and the soreness of his body. He'd fought back nausea, failing only one more time before releasing his stomach contents onto the earth. It was almost certain he was concussed, and it was only by the grace of God that he was standing.

But how to subdue Gordon? Without his gun, he couldn't demand Gordon's compliance. Gordon didn't appear to be armed, aside from bear spray, which Wade also had. He wasn't thrilled with the idea of a potential duel with that high a concentration of pepper spray. It would do more than the average law enforcement spray. It would steal their breath, their ability to function and very possibly even their eyesight if one caught it full in the face. To release it on Gordon was to release it on Aaliyah and himself. The spray would permeate the area. It would be a last ditch option.

No. He had to think of something else, and that meant more than likely a physical altercation. And then, Wade would need to pray that Gordon didn't have a concealed weapon that wasn't accounted for.

"Why did you attack me in my own home that night?" Aaliyah's question was open-ended and demanded more of an answer than yes or no.

Atta girl! Wade mentally cheered. He calculated the distance between him and Gordon.

"Attack you?" Gordon's voice rose an octave. He paced in front of Aaliyah, the first time that he might be getting agitated. "I never set out to attack you that night. I was so bewildered by the news—and then, I didn't believe it yet either."

"DNA doesn't lie," Aaliyah retorted.

That's right, Wade mentally coached her, *keep him talking*.

"No, but people do." Gordon's retort was met with a sniff from Aaliyah. She leveled a thin smile at him.

"But you overheard the conversation about my relationship to Deborah Platt. So there was no reason to assume it was a lie."

"You're right, of course." Gordon paused in front of Aaliyah's form. She had to be so uncomfortable with her ankles tied and her hands restrained behind her back. Gordon continued. "But in truth, I wasn't in your home to hurt you. My only goal was to search your things—see if there was anything you had to corroborate Marlowe's claim that you were Deborah's infant. Then you came home early, and it was like a parade of people. That old man—"

"Charlie," Aaliyah gritted through clenched teeth.

"He didn't deserve to be wrapped up in this. He'd already been a suspect after I killed Deborah. His souvenir shop and the arrowhead bracelets." Gordon snorted. "I wasn't dumb enough to get them locally. But it was a good diversion for the police to be suspicious of him."

Wade noticed Aaliyah's face redden. *Stay calm*, he mentally urged her. He eyed a boulder about three yards away and to his east. If he could get behind it without being noticed, he'd be within distance of being able to come at Gordon from behind.

"And then?" Aaliyah prompted. Her eyes lifted for a brief second and met Wade's. He lifted his finger to his lips.

Gordon rubbed his hand over his chin, a sign of agitation. Wade's concern mounted. If Gordon were to finally get emotional, then he could become impulsive. For now, it appeared he had a plan and felt in control of the situation, and that was exactly how Wade needed him to be.

"Then Marlowe stopped by. At this point, I didn't want to kill either of you. I needed more information." Gordon was so calculated it was chilling.

Wade positioned himself on the balls of his feet. The next moment Gordon spoke, he would make a dodge for the boulder.

Gordon cooperated. "Then Marlowe left, you came down the hall, there was no way out without you seeing me and— you know the rest." Gordon offered a wild wave of his hand.

Wade lurched forward, willing his feet to avoid any sticks or debris that might give away his presence. He ducked behind the boulder, his chest rising and falling in carefully controlled breaths. He was only about fifteen feet away now. He just needed the right opening to make his move.

"So!" Gordon squatted in front of Aaliyah again. Eye contact seemed to be important to him, and Wade could tell it was a way for Gordon to assure himself that he had control over Aaliyah. That she was listening to him, capitulating to him. "That's that."

"No." Aaliyah shook her head. She glanced at the boulder Wade hid behind. He gave a quick shake of his head.

Ignore me. Don't draw attention.

Aaliyah focused on Gordon. "Then you abducted me. You strangled me and—"

"I did not strangle you!" Gordon launched to his feet. A thin thread of steel laced his voice. She'd offended him. "There are ways to gently apply pressure to induce someone into an unconscious state. You know this, Aaliyah."

Aaliyah gave a short laugh. "You strangled me," she repeated.

Wade could see what she was doing, and she was smart. Gordon grew agitated. He kicked a rock and sent it flying into the trees.

"Only because I wanted to—" Gordon bit off his words.

Aaliyah leaned forward, taunting him, claiming his attention. "Because you thought I'd suddenly want to become your daughter? You'd still get half the family you always wanted with Deborah?"

Gordon took a strong step toward Aaliyah. He towered over her, but she didn't shrink against the tree she sat by. Instead, she maintained her stubborn position.

Wade was impressed.

Gordon bent at the waist, pointing toward the empty graves. "Did you want to end up here?" He spit the words.

He was losing control. "I was trying to spare you, Aaliyah! We have too much history anyway, and we could have been a *family*!" he declared with vehemence. "But no! You had to ruin that too. So now? I have no other recourse. None. I've considered all my options, but there is no other choice. Deborah set this in motion. You can blame your mother."

"And how many other women have you killed because of the failure of this imaginary family?" Aaliyah mocked.

Without warning, Gordon swung; his palm slapped against Aaliyah's face, and she cried out.

Wade launched at Gordon, his only weapon a quickly breathed prayer.

Aaliyah's face throbbed at the impact of Gordon's hand. She'd half expected it due to her taunting of him, but it still stunned her.

She saw the blur through her watery eyes and smarting face as Wade launched himself at Gordon. It took the ranger by surprise as Wade engulfed him from behind. The two men went down in a scuffle of legs and arms. Gordon flipped Wade over onto his back and delivered a well-aimed blow to Wade's side.

Wade grunted. It was apparent he was not at his full form. Dried blood from the accident painted the side of his face. He had to be concussed for as long as he'd been unconscious. That he had hiked here at all was astounding in and of itself.

Aaliyah wasted no time in trying to free herself from her bonds. The plastic tie around her wrist already dug into her skin, so as she scraped it along the bark of the tree, she could feel it rubbing her wrists raw.

Wade managed to twist from beneath Gordon's bulky form. He leveled a fist at Gordon's face, but Gordon dodged.

A smile snaked across his face as he and Wade circled each other like animals preparing to pounce.

"Yeahhhhh, here you are." Gordon's hand dropped to the bear spray at his side. "Playing the hero again, eh, Marlowe?"

Wade's body was tense and prepared.

Aaliyah noticed Wade paying close attention to Gordon's grip on the bear spray. "I'm no hero, but I'm not a killer like you."

"Ouch." Gordon sneered. He unclipped the can.

"You'll only hurt yourself if you use that." Wade tipped his head to the can.

Aaliyah grimaced. Wade did not have the situation under control by any means, and she was worthless to help him.

Wade staggered and Aaliyah could see his eyes were glassy. He was in no condition to fight. If Gordon delivered a blow to Wade's head, that alone could kill him if he was already concussed.

Aaliyah worked frantically at her bound wrists. She could feel the blood running from the tie down her hands. The tree was doing little to break her bonds, and her feet were also too tight to give her any leverage to break the plastic strap.

Before Gordon could deploy the bear spray, Wade flew at him.

A scream ripped from Aaliyah's throat.

Wade's arms wrapped around Gordon's legs, dropping him to the earth. The bear spray rolled and bounced away from them. Grunts ensued, and Aaliyah struggled harder to free herself from her bonds.

Gordon wrestled against Wade's weight, and Wade leveled an uppercut to Gordon's jaw.

"It's over!" Wade shouted.

Gordon hefted off the ground, shoving his elbows into the dirt and twisting to roll from beneath Wade's weight. Wade must have expected the movement as he rolled with Gordon, narrowly dodging a blow aimed at his head.

"Gordon, stop!" Aaliyah yelled, resorting to pleading for Wade's life. If there was an ounce of loyalty left in her coworker—in her friend—she hoped her cries would trigger it in Gordon.

She was ignored, and Gordon shoved Wade off of him. He bent, and in a swift motion, there was the glistening of a knife. He'd pulled it from his boot, and now he held it away from himself, ready to use on Wade's next advance.

"Don't do it," Gordon warned Wade.

Wade managed to stumble to his feet. "You're going to kill me?" Wade goaded. "Then what? Kill Aaliyah? It's over, Gordon, regardless of what you do to us. You can't keep on with this."

Gordon growled deep in his throat. "You know nothing, Marlowe. You may have opened my eyes to what really happened to Deborah's baby, but you've done nothing to influence me."

"Gordon, please stop and listen!" Aaliyah cried.

Gordon glanced at her, hoisting the blade more definitively in front of him. He and Wade were at a standoff, and Aaliyah knew unless Wade was swift on his feet, that the odds were stacked in Gordon's favor.

"I deserve a family." Gordon gritted the words through clenched teeth.

"Is this how you get one?" Wade swept his arm over the empty graves. "Trial and error? Befriend a woman who has no family and see if she'll measure up to Deborah? See if she'll have children with you? Then what? Kill them when they fall short?"

"Don't say her name!" Gordon swiped the knife at Wade.

Wade arched his back and leaped away, preventing the blade from slashing at his stomach.

"*She* deserted *me*. She deserted Aaliyah." Gordon's protest spoke to the turbulence inside of him. If she could find a good reason, Aaliyah would almost pity him at this moment.

Her coworker whom she'd worked alongside for two years had never shown signs of being lonely. He had only been kind and generous. There was no evidence that he was a killer. But for the course of her life, Gordon had been fostering a dream that distorted and transitioned into something evil. Something dark. That something, Aaliyah had to believe, was what Deborah Platt had tried to save her from when she'd left Aaliyah as a newborn in the alley. Before she'd been murdered for having lost her baby, before she'd been left dead in the wilderness for failing to provide the perfect equation of a family for Gordon.

"Gordon?" Aaliyah tried to get his attention.

Gordon ignored her, his glare fixed on Wade and unyielding in its cold intent. "It never should have been like this," he growled.

Wade stumbled, his eyes momentarily going blank.

Aaliyah screamed his name to jerk him back to awareness.

It was too late.

Gordon hurtled forward, collapsing Wade's legs beneath him and taking him to the ground. His knee pressed into Wade's chest, Gordon held the knife to Wade's throat.

The whites of Wade's eyes were clear, his focus coming back into the stark realization that he was about to die.

No, no, no!

Aliyah threw herself forward, bound hands and feet inhibiting any interceding she could offer.

"Gordon, don't!" Her scream ripped through the air just as the resounding blast of a gun pierced the wilderness.

The next second hung in the air as if on pause.

Aaliyah lay on her side on the ground, her mouth open in a silent cry.

Wade's body went limp beneath Gordon's, his head lolling to the side, his eyes closing.

Gordon held his position, knife poised at Wade's throat, his left hand pressing down on Wade's shoulder, his body straddling Wade's.

Then, Aaliyah saw it. The slow spread of red across Gordon's chest. Blood seeping through his khaki uniform. Shock crossed the man's face. He dropped the knife and fell off Wade.

Gordon's shoulder hit the ground, and he lay on his side. Mere feet separated them, Aaliyah still bound and Gordon's eyes wide with consternation and surprise. His mouth opened and then closed, then opened again.

"We could have been a family," he gasped. "Deborah ruined it all."

"No, Gordon." Hot tears raced down Aaliyah's face. She hated Gordon for all he had done, for the wickedness he had inflicted on others, including her birth mother. But she also broke for the man she had called her friend. The man who had taught her how to be a good ranger, to love the wilderness, to care for its wildlife, its waters, its biology.

"No, Gordon," she repeated through tears. "*You* ruined it all."

A shout.

Footsteps.

Aaliyah saw Buck's form bend over Wade, feeling for a pulse. Peaches bounded toward her, licking her face and whining. Buck, apparently appeased that Wade was stable for the moment, spun and sank on the ground between Aaliyah and Gordon.

"What have I done? What have I done?" he moaned, tears streaking down his weathered face. Buck managed to have the presence of mind to cut through Aaliyah's bonds, and she sat up, careful not to aggravate the open skin and cuts on her wrists made while trying to break free.

She reached for Buck, who bent over Gordon's still body. "You had to. He was going to kill Wade."

"But he's my brother!" Buck's words were hoarse with emotion. "My *brother*!" He scrambled to find a pulse. "He's still alive." The gravity of the situation became clear to Aaliyah as Buck tended to Gordon—the man who didn't deserve to live. And yet, Aaliyah couldn't wish for Buck to live with the truth he'd shot and killed his own brother.

"Give me your phone." Aaliyah reached for the sat phone even as Buck pulled it from the clip at his waist. "I'll call in a medical evac."

It was as though the realization of it all came barreling down on the sheriff as he took his knife and cut away Gordon's shirt. He stripped from his own shirt and, clad only in a white undershirt, balled up the flannel and pressed it against Gordon's chest wound. Buck's shot had not been fatal—at least not yet.

Aaliyah called in the situation. Once reassured help was on the way, she returned to Buck and also to Wade, who had rolled into a sitting position, his head held between his hands, elbows propped on his knees.

Buck tossed words at Aaliyah. "Gordon was behind this?

He was the Arrowhead Killer?" Without waiting for an answer, he asked, "Why, Gordon?"

Aaliyah wanted desperately to relieve Buck, to comfort him, to give him answers—however awful they may be—to his question of why. But first, Wade was a priority. She hurried to his side, Peaches on her heels.

Wade lifted his head from his hands as Aaliyah kneeled next to him, brushing back dark hair from his forehead. "You came," she whispered.

Wade offered her a low, weak chuckle. "Just remember everything I did to save you when we're all healthy and happy again. You owe *me* a coffee this time."

"I'll gladly get you a coffee." Aaliyah couldn't help herself. She leaned in and pressed a kiss to his temple—the side that wasn't covered in dried blood from the accident.

Wade shifted his attention back to Buck. "How'd you know to come here?"

Buck glanced at Wade, and a look passed between the men that Aaliyah couldn't interpret. Buck turned back to Gordon, but answered as he did so. "I knew you and Aaliyah were coming out here—I didn't feel good about it. I was already on my way to check in on you when I saw Peaches running down the road."

Peaches. She *had* done it! Aaliyah reached for her dog and hugged her around her furry neck.

Buck held his shirt on the gunshot wound he'd inflicted. "Hang in there, Gordon. I'm so sorry. I'm so sorry."

Aaliyah and Wade exchanged looks. Wade cleared his throat, wincing as he did. "You had to, Buck. He was going to kill me. He was going to kill Aaliyah."

"I don't understand. I don't understand any of it." Buck shook his head.

Aaliyah moved from Wade, nearer to Gordon and Buck.

She reached out, grasping on to her godfather's shoulder in an attempt to offer comfort. "It's nobody's fault, Buck." She tried to reassure him. "You couldn't have known."

"That's just it, though." Buck's expression was pained. It contorted into an emotional type of agony that Aaliyah wasn't able to read. Grief? Guilt?

Buck pulled his hand from hers, almost as though he couldn't bear to touch her, let alone have her touch him. "I've been so blind. So very, very blind." He shook his head. "I should have known all along—I should have faced the truth of it…"

"Buck." There was a warning tone to Wade's comment.

Buck bit back the rest of his words.

Aaliyah looked between them, Wade holding his head, pale from the trauma of the day, and Buck applying pressure to his brother's wound.

Aaliyah was beginning to be worried now. She frowned. "What's going on?"

Buck lifted agonized eyes to hers. "In my heart—I think I always suspected the unknown woman to be Deborah. I just—there wasn't any way to be sure."

Wade interrupted. "We can talk about this later. Right now, focus on Gordon."

Aaliyah frowned. Was Wade actually that concerned if Gordon made it? She would be fine if he died. Did that make her an awful human being? Did it disappoint God that she wished death on a criminal? Not just a criminal, a murderer?

"But now I know," Buck continued as if he hadn't heard Wade. "Now I know everything for sure."

A cold numbness began to creep up Aaliyah's spine. "Wade?" She demanded he look at her. He did, and what she saw there sent another wave of anxiety through her.

"What's going on?" It was obvious there was still information she was not privy to. Information that both Buck and Wade were withholding—Wade more vehemently than Buck.

Buck's words croaked through emotion that must have clogged his throat. "I caused this. All of this."

"How?" Aaliyah insisted.

Buck's voice grew distant and even more pained than it already was. "Deborah—and I—" He met Aaliyah's eyes then, his watery with unshed tears. He reached with one free hand into his back jeans pocket and tugged out a folded piece of paper. His fingers smeared some of Gordon's blood across it. "Wade gave me this—just yesterday. I guess I always knew, I just..."

"Buck!" Wade's voice was sharper than Aaliyah had expected. She froze at the command in his voice. Wade looked between them, a pleading expression filling his eyes. "Please. Not here. Not now. Let's—let's focus on Gordon and the evac." Wade didn't mention he needed medical care too, but the way his eyes were glassy, Aaliyah was concerned he'd pass out soon himself. But for the moment? For the moment, she didn't care.

Aaliyah snatched the paper from Buck's hand and opened it, staring down at it.

Wade's heavy sigh did nothing to ease her anxiety.

Her eyes skimmed the page. It was a record of hits in the DNA database that linked back to Aaliyah's DNA profile. Deborah Platt was listed as mother, but in the paternity line, there was also a name. A remarkably familiar name that knocked Aaliyah backward and away from Buck and from Wade.

She threw the paper, and it landed on Wade's chest.

"Aaliyah, wait. You need to understand." He begged her, but she was in no mood for his mournful pleas.

Aaliyah scrambled to her feet. "You knew, didn't you?" She demanded. "Both of you knew!"

"Only since yesterday when Wade gave me that." Buck held up one hand, palm toward her.

Aaliyah glared down at Wade. "And how long did you know?"

He struggled, obviously battling between the whole truth and withholding for whatever good reason he thought he had. Wade reached for her. "Aaliyah, I…"

"No. You can get medical care by yourself," she half shouted at Wade as tears clogged her throat, and then she leveled a look at Buck that she hoped would spear him where it hurt the most. In his heart. "And *you* will *never* be my father."

THIRTEEN

The town buzzed with the excitement of it all. Maybe it was exciting for them, but for Wade, it was perhaps the worst way this case could have come to a semi-close. Yes, he'd identified the cold case victim: Deborah Platt. He'd identified her daughter as Aaliyah. He'd even had the success of matching Aaliyah's DNA to Buck's—and that had gone over like a birthday party without a cake.

Wade lay in the hospital bed, recovering from his concussion, an IV dripping and the heart monitor beeping steadily to remind him he was still alive. He'd touched base with his office in Helena and updated them on Gordon's arrest. The fact Gordon had made it out of the Bob still breathing was astounding until Wade considered the fact that the sinful part of him wished the man had just died. God forgive him. Justice was the Lord's. Wade had reminded himself of that often, especially during his sister's murder trial.

"Time for company?" Buck poked his head into the room.

Wade eyed the sheriff for a moment before giving him a short nod.

Buck entered, hesitation registering on his entire body.

He slouched onto a chair next to the bed. "Glad to see you're going to be all right," he observed.

"Concussions heal." Wade's answer was curt. He wasn't happy with Buck. He wasn't happy with the way Buck had gone about telling Aaliyah he was her birth father. It lacked consideration and gentility, and in the chaos of what happened—it was almost cruel.

"I know I botched it up." Buck must have read Wade's face. There was something in the man's eyes Wade couldn't interpret, so he waited. Buck drew a deep breath and then let it out, tapping his foot on the linoleum floor. "I almost killed my brother, Wade—I wasn't thinking straight."

Wade had to give the man some grace. "You saved my life taking a shot at Gordon," Wade acquiesced. "I'm grateful for that."

Buck sniffed. "Yeah. Well. Gordon's going to survive after all. He'll go down for Deborah's murder and the others."

Wade waited. Buck was here for a reason, and a foreboding in Wade's gut told him he wasn't going to like it.

"When you showed me that paper—that I was—that Aaliyah was my daughter, I didn't know how to process it."

Wade had shown the paper with the DNA results to Buck two days before he and Aaliyah had gone out to the Bob. He hadn't felt it was his place to tell Aaliyah—now he wished he had.

"But you didn't know about me from the get-go," Buck surmised. "Or did you?"

"No." This was the part Wade knew Aaliyah wouldn't like—and the part he hadn't even filled Buck in on. He'd been in communication with his assistant back in Helena, who was doing some background research in case they turned up something to help identify the Arrowhead Killer.

He had asked her to run Aaliyah's DNA against law enforcement records—on a hunch. Something about Buck had always been a bit off to him, but when the results came through, he had been reluctant to move on them.

Wade answered Buck. "We ran Aaliyah's DNA against our records. Of course, we got a hit."

Buck drew back, confused. "What made you do that?"

Wade eyed him. "C'mon. Seriously?"

Buck reddened.

"Call it a gut feeling, but the way everything was developing, you weren't doing a great job of looking innocent, Buck. I'm also thorough in my investigations. I don't assume people in law enforcement are above their own secrets. If it's in a database, I'm going to use it."

Buck nodded.

That was all Wade needed to know. "You've always been close to the investigation on the cold case—you've been close to Aaliyah. The dots are there, Buck. I just needed to connect them. Did Gordon know? All these years, that you were the one who'd gotten Deborah pregnant?"

Buck groaned and leaned forward, his elbows on his knees, his thick fingers jutting through his peppery gray hair. "No. It was a classic tale of a one-night stand. After Deborah told me, I cut ties. Paid her to keep her quiet. I didn't want anything to tarnish my career, and she needed the money."

"Stand-up guy," Wade muttered.

Buck raised his eyes and was more direct than Wade expected him to be. "I was a cocky cop, that's what I was. I never told Gordon. To my knowledge, neither did Deborah. She was just—an expecting single mother."

"Gordon probably would've killed you had he known," Wade theorized.

Buck held his head between his hands, his voice muffled. "This is out of hand."

Wade eyed him. "And yet I feel like you're still not being one-hundred-percent truthful with me. What aren't you telling me, Buck?"

Buck lifted his head in question.

Wade was having none of it. "How did you not know the baby found in the alley behind the church was yours? How did you not know that the woman found a few months later was Deborah? How did you not know about Gordon?"

Buck reared back, his eyes flashing. "Hold up there, son. It's not as easy as all that!"

"No? Then explain it to me."

"There's nothing to explain!" Buck roared. "It happened. It was what it was. I'm not proud of it, but things fell into place for Aaliyah and her life and—I had no idea the body was Deborah any more than it was some other random female. Gordon? There were absolutely no signs."

Wade ignored the pounding in his head. "So then, what aren't you telling me?"

Buck opened his mouth to retort and then snapped it shut. He ran his hand over his mouth and then his finger under his nose. He stood, marching to the window, hands on his hips. Buck spun around to address Wade. "No one has seen Aaliyah since yesterday, Wade."

"What?" Wade pushed himself straighter in the hospital bed. Warning ripples shot through him. "What happened?"

"After they evac'ed us out of the Bob, Aaliyah went to the hospital and got checked out. She was released—close to midnight. But no one has seen her since. Her parents said she has Peaches, but her truck is gone, and she shut off her cell phone, so her GPS isn't on."

"What did you expect her to have done?" Wade shot back.

"Now, don't go blamin' me," Buck snapped in return.

Wade glared at him.

"Okay." Buck drew back and lowered his shoulders. "Fine. It's my fault."

Wade pushed back the hospital blanket. He picked at the tape on his IV.

"What're you doing?" Buck started forward.

Wade snorted. "Going to find Aaliyah."

"Hold on there." Buck laid his hand on Wade's shoulder. Wade shook it off. "Now, wait up!" Buck directed sternly. "She's a grown woman, and my brother is cuffed to a hospital bed with a gunshot wound in his chest. He isn't a threat to her."

"Nope." Wade pulled the IV from his elbow and grabbed tissues from the box, pressing it against the blood that beaded. "But she's traumatized, Buck. In just about every way she can be. And I won't let it happen again."

"Let what happen again?" Buck frowned, stepping back as Wade swung his legs from the bed.

Wade reached for his jeans that were folded in the chair beside the bed. His head throbbed, but he'd deal with it. The hospital was going to release him later today anyway. What was the difference of a few hours?

Buck's firm grip on Wade's shoulder made him pause. He looked up at the older man whose eyes now resembled Aaliyah's in a stunning way that Wade would have otherwise never seen. Hazel. Emotional. Independent.

"What are you afraid of happening again?" Buck pressed.

Visions of Amy flooded Wade's mind. Their falling out. The betrayal in his sister's voice. He had judged her decisions. She'd been hurt, and rightfully so. He'd been angry.

Then she'd been murdered. Pure coincidence and a one-in-a-million chance that it would have happened. But it had.

Wade dressed himself and disposed of the hospital gown. "My sister. She was murdered."

Buck said nothing, but the shock on his face told Wade he'd heard, and he was beginning to understand.

Wade reached for his T-shirt, tugging it over his head. "I made a promise not only to get justice for families living without answers, but to protect them too. I wasn't there for my sister. I won't let that happen again. Even if we think Aaliyah is safe from Gordon—is she safe from the effects of all this?" He met Buck's gaze, and he meant for his question to be sincere.

Buck's eyes filled with emotion. "All right. I hear you."

Wade hefted a determined breath. "We owe Aaliyah this. We owe it to her, Buck."

The older man gave a swift nod. "Let's get you checked out of the hospital."

Wade and Buck paused outside the hospital before crossing the parking lot to Buck's vehicle. Buck was on his phone with Aaliyah's dad, the speaker on so Wade could hear too.

"Do you have any idea where she could have gone?" Buck asked.

There was tense worry in the reply. "The only place she ever goes when she needs to be alone is to the Bob. But she always takes the eastern route, and with everything that happened, I can't figure she'd go back there. Not now anyway."

"No." Buck shook his head.

Wade agreed, though he remained silent, tapping his fingers on his leg and willing away the continued dull throb of his concussion.

"I already called the ranger station, and she never checked in there either," Aaliyah's dad supplied.

Buck's brows drew together. "That's not like Aaliyah."

"She doesn't want to be found," Wade supplied.

"Maybe we should leave her be," Buck suggested, a hesitant look cast in Wade's direction.

Wade and Aaliyah's father said, "No!" simultaneously with a similar amount of emphatic surety.

"She's a grown adult. She's a ranger, and she knows her way around the wilderness." Buck's argument drew a scowl from Wade.

"You really think she's in a mindset to make wise decisions?" Wade countered.

"How do I know?" Buck retorted. He slapped his palm against the fender of the parked vehicle.

"Gordon would know." Aaliyah's father's voice sliced through the air, and Buck and Wade froze.

"What do you mean?" Wade demanded.

Aaliyah's father's sigh reverberated over the airways. "Gordon knows all the places she would go. She worked with him day in and out for over two years."

"That's assuming she actually went out to the wilderness," Wade countered.

"She did," Aaliyah's father replied emphatically. "I know she did. It's what she does. The wilderness is her refuge, and her refuge has been tarnished by everything that has gone on. She might not think of it this way, but Aaliyah will need to go back. To experience it on her terms and regain an element of normalcy."

"And you think Gordon would know where she went?" Wade restated, dreading the very notion of engaging Gordon in a conversation that included Aaliyah, let alone maybe had her welfare hinging on it.

"I believe he'd have a good idea, yes."

Buck shook his head and speared Wade with a dark look. "I'm not giving Gordon the satisfaction of having any control over us finding Aaliyah."

"We may not have a choice," Wade retorted.

"Gordon can barely talk right now. He's fortunate to even be conscious and off a ventilator!" Buck protested more. "I say we give Aaliyah a full twenty-four hours at least. In law enforcement, we give missing adults forty-eight more often than not. People need to get away."

"But not to the wilderness and not alone in the wilderness," Wade countered.

"I agree with Marlowe," Aaliyah's father spoke over the phone.

"Fine," Buck agreed. "We'll go back into the hospital and ask Gordon." His reaction was dark and resistant as he bent toward the phone. "We'll find your daughter." He ended the call.

Wade moved to follow the sheriff, but as he met up with Buck, he put a hand out to stop Buck from charging back into the hospital and to his brother's room.

Buck eyed the hand on his arm.

Wade had no intention of letting Buck off that easily. "If you know something that could hurt Aaliyah…" He leveled a black look on the man.

Buck's responding chuckle was resigned. "*Everything* I know could hurt Aaliyah." He started back toward the medical facility. "All I've ever done is hurt Aaliyah."

FOURTEEN

A litany of machines beeped and pumped and croaked in Gordon's hospital room. He was in the ICU, and the medical staff was resistant to allowing both Buck and Wade entry into his room. It didn't seem to matter that he was a serial killer. He still received the same treatment as other patients, and medical care was unbiased. Regardless, Wade convinced them that in spite of the fact he wasn't immediate family, he was law enforcement, and this was crucial to the case. Now they stood over Gordon, staring down at the man whose face was bruised from his fight with Wade, and whose body was weakened by the gunshot wound his brother had inflicted on him.

Gordon opened his eyes, taking in first Wade and then coming to rest on Buck. He narrowed them, and his voice was hoarse when he spoke. "Come to finish the job?"

"Don't put this on me, Gordon." Buck crossed his arms over his chest. "You know what you did."

Gordon closed his eyes. His breathing was labored, and it was obvious he didn't have much energy to form words let alone argue.

Wade took a step toward the bed, anxious to get answers. This wasn't the time for the two brothers to duke it out verbally, and there was no coming back for Gordon.

He'd murdered. He'd hunted and stalked Aaliyah as if she were his prey, as though she somehow belonged to him. And even now, somehow, after he'd been apprehended, it still felt like Aaliyah was in Gordon's clutches.

Buck held out a hand to stop Wade. He leaned over his brother. "Tell me where she is."

Gordon opened his eyes again. A small smile twisted his mouth. "You lost her already?"

Buck drew in a controlled breath, but his expression was severe. He flicked the blanket that was over Gordon's chest. It was a simple gesture but carried threat all the same. "Where would Aaliyah go if she wanted to disappear?"

Gordon turned his head away from Buck, his cheek resting on the pillow, his oxygen cord stretched across his neck.

Buck leaned in closer. "Tell me."

Gordon turned back to his brother, his eyes clouded by the drugs they had him on.

Wade reached for Buck's arm. "He's not even with it."

"Yes, he is." Buck shrugged off Wade's hand. "He's pretending. The same way he has pulled the wool over my eyes for twenty-five years."

Gordon blinked a few times then winced. "Why would she disappear? I'm in here. There's nothing to be afraid of anymore." Gordon's light cough caused him to grimace.

Wade pushed in between Buck and Gordon. He didn't feel like dancing around the emotional baggage the two brothers staring down sixty plus years of sibling-hood shared. He wanted basic answers.

"Where does she go in the Bob to get away from things?" Wade demanded.

Gordon shifted his eyes to look at Wade. His brows furrowed even deeper than they already were. His peppery hair stood up on end, and his chin was covered in unshaven whiskers. "To get away? Aaliyah never needed to get away until you came along."

Wade was finished with these games, but he was interrupted when a nurse entered the room. She made movements to check Gordon's vitals, examine the machine, all while Wade and Gordon refused to break their stare. With gazes locked, it was apparent they were at odds. The nurse looked between them and then at Buck.

"Two more minutes is all. The patient needs to rest." She exited the room.

"Yes," Gordon whispered. "The patient needs to rest."

"C'mon, Marlowe." Buck tapped Wade's arm. "He's not going to help us."

Gordon glared at his brother, his words raspy. "Are you really her father?" He lifted his arm enough to clank the handcuff on his wrist with the rail on the bed.

Buck blanched.

"Yeah, I heard you after you shot me. DNA? You're the jerk who left Deborah to fend for herself?"

"Don't you dare blame this on me," Buck snarled.

"Enough!" Wade held his hands up. He turned and pushed Buck away from the hospital bed with his palms on Buck's chest. "You're right," he said with earnestness. "Gordon isn't going to help us." Wade shot a glance over his shoulder at the man, who had already closed his eyes. He still had a feeling Gordon was listening though, so he hoped his plan would work. "You would've made a better father than Gordon anyway, Buck." Wade gave Buck a look that indicated he should play along. "It's too bad things didn't work out for you to raise Aaliyah."

Buck glanced at his brother, pressing his lips together. It was obvious the next words hurt him to speak. "Honestly? Sometimes I wondered if Gordon might've been the bigger man. But I guess—" He swallowed hard, and Wade could see what this was costing Buck. "I guess we'll never know now." Buck spun on his heel and hiked from the room.

Wade followed, but Gordon's voice, low and wheezing, stopped him—just as he'd hoped.

"Go west, young man," Gordon rasped. He offered Wade a thin smile. "West meets south, you know?"

Aaliyah lay on the bank by the river. It had taken everything in her willpower to not pass out when she dragged herself to sit against a tree. Her ankle stabbed with angry shots of pain. It was Murphy's Law she'd head to her beloved wilderness to escape, to think, and end up twisting her ankle on shale. She knew better. All the way around, she knew better. This was what happened when emotion drove a person instead of common sense.

Peaches paced around her, whining, licking at her forehead, before she finally lay down beside Aaliyah. Her head up and her ears perked, Peaches kept guard.

She needed to rest a bit and then figure out how to splint her ankle before somehow managing the trek back to her truck. This was stupid 101, and Aaliyah knew it. She'd known the errors she was making when she'd set out for this section of the Bob. The irony? The only person who knew she liked to escape here was Gordon.

A tear escaped the corner of her eye. She felt like a victim, and she didn't want to feel that way. Victims were powerless over their circumstances, but wasn't that where she was now? All the villains in her life had influenced her negatively, and her reaction had now landed her on the bank of the Flathead River with a broken ankle and no rescue in sight. She was a walking calamity and a magnet for trouble all in the last two weeks. Before this? Life had been blessed. She was doing what she loved, with a dog she adored, a coworker she trusted and parents and a godfather who had—up until then—never abandoned her.

"It's come full circle, hasn't it?" Aaliyah reached for Peaches. The dog whined and nuzzled her hand with her wet nose. "Abandoned behind a church in a back alley to this. Alone in the wilderness with a broken ankle. How do I reconcile it all?" Aaliyah's whisper was a serious prayer as she lifted her eyes to the vast blue sky above her. Tips of pine trees seemed like they could touch the clouds as Aaliyah lay on her back looking up.

She moaned as she rolled onto her side. Peaches scurried to her feet and stood over Aaliyah. Telling Peaches to go find help this time was not an option. In an area of the Bob less frequented, Peaches wouldn't know where to go, and their familiar stomping grounds were miles and miles away.

Aaliyah pushed herself into a sitting position, staring at her ankle. If she could splint it, maybe she could manage to get to the truck. Or a stick long enough to lean on might provide enough stability for her to hop on one foot. She didn't fight the tears as they fell. She was broken. Broken everywhere, it seemed, and for the first time in forever, she had lost the will to fight.

Fighting through a broken ankle was one thing. But how did one fight through a broken heart?

The truck bounced over washboards and ruts, taking sharp curves with care and exacerbating the pain in Wade's head. Wild horses wouldn't have kept him back in Park Springs, but this drive to the Bob on the western pass just might be the death of him. But then he'd be no good to Aaliyah. No good to anyone.

"How much longer?" he growled, partly because of the

pain and partly because Buck had said nothing almost the entire trip.

"Don't know. It depends on where she pulled off. It's a maze out here, you know that. It's not just one road and oops, there, we passed her truck." The sarcasm in Buck's words proved to Wade that Buck was as concerned as he was. Gordon may have sent them on a wild-goose chase. Aaliyah could be halfway across the state by now if she hadn't come to the Bob. She could be in the Bob but at a totally different location. A different pass. She could have driven to Hungry Horse or Seeley Lake or—

"You sure Gordon said west?" Buck interrupted Wade's internal assessment.

Wade held on to the door for support as the truck bounced. His brain felt jostled and sore. "He said to go west. That west meets south."

Buck blew out a puff of air. "Taking his word for it doesn't give me much comfort. But the western road out to the Bob does lead to the south fork of the Flathead."

"And Gordon likes to have the last word," Wade concluded. "So we gave it to him. He can be the hero in his own head if he needs to be. The better one of the two of you."

"Thanks a lot," Buck muttered.

"It makes sense Aaliyah would come to the river," Wade continued. "Her dad said she likes to fly fish. So one plus one makes two, I guess."

"It's a start," Buck retorted.

Wade eyed him. "You're afraid to face her aren't you?"

Buck gave him a sideways glance. "Of course I am! If she came out here, she came to get away from me, not have me come chasing her down."

Wade didn't reply. Buck had a valid point, but still, Wade had no good feeling about Aaliyah taking off without telling anyone. It went against who she was as a ranger. It told him she wasn't thinking with anything but her emotions—and emotions could put a person into tricky spots really fast.

"What's that up ahead?" Wade leaned forward, bracing his palm against the dash, and pointed with his free hand.

"I see it too." Buck noted the pull-off that merged into a meadow bordered by pines and a lush, green valley. Beyond that was a dip in the landscape and plant life that was rich with health, evidence of water. "The river's that way." Buck nodded in the direction of the valley. "This would be a logical place for her to come and park. She'd need to trek back a ways, but there's good fishing back in there. Not a lot of bear either, from what I've heard."

"Let's check it out."

Within minutes, they were hiking across the meadow at a steady pace. If Aaliyah was out here, she could have already hiked a few miles in. Finding her out here could very well be like finding a needle in a haystack.

"Aaliyah!" Wade cupped his hands around his mouth.

"Aaliyah!" Buck echoed.

"Let's spread out a bit. You head over there, and I'll go straight. Stay within shouting distance." Wade's instruction to Buck was met with swift agreement. Buck veered off to the left, while Wade continued his trajectory.

A moment later, he noted something black charging through the grass toward him. Wade stilled, eyeing the form cautiously. Bear could move far more swiftly that most gave them credit, yet this animal was nowhere near the size of a grizzly or even a black bear. It also didn't have the brawn of a bear in full charge.

"Peaches!" Wade called, almost certain it was Aaliyah's dog. He turned and spotted Buck. "Hey, Buck! Over here!" He was mauled after all, but by Peaches as she catapulted into him with a happy grin on her muzzle. Her haunches wiggled back and forth as Wade bent over the dog. "Hey, girl. Hey, Peaches. Where's your mama, huh? Where's Aaliyah?"

Buck jogged through the meadow in the direction of the river, and Wade joined him, Peaches beside him. "Take me to Aaliyah, girl." Whether the Lab understood him or not, Wade wasn't sure, but they crossed the meadow, and the ground transitioned from hard-packed earth covered in grasses to shale and rock leading down to a sparkling river. It was beautiful. Pine and spruce lined the banks. The water was crystal clear mountain water, with pools and riffles doing the tango around rocks perched in its middle.

But it was the form lying prostrate on the bank that caught Wade's attention. It had also caught Buck's.

"Aaliyah!" Buck shouted.

Her arm came up in a half-hearted wave, and it was that moment that Wade knew every instinct in his gut had been correct. Not everything was okay.

When he reached Aaliyah's side, stones crunched beneath his boots as he knelt beside her. Buck wasn't far behind, and he reached the other side of her just as Peaches flopped on her stomach, content that she had once again retrieved help for her mistress in need.

Aaliyah's hazel eyes looked first at Buck and then at Wade. Wade could see pain etched in her face, and her ivory skin was even paler, the smattering of freckles across her nose even more prominent.

"So much for getting out for some fresh air," she quipped.

"What happened?" Wade asked as his gaze swept over her body. "You trying to dance on one foot?"

"Hardly." Aaliyah had yet to address Buck, and Wade wasn't sure how to read that. If he was the worst of two evils in her eyes, or if she was simply not caring due to the pain. "I think I might have fractured my ankle." She waved her fingers at her right leg.

Buck shifted beside her, but Aaliyah's hand lifted and she touched his shoulder. "Please." Her voice softened but was laced with a hard edge that stilled even Wade. She looked between them. "Do what we need to get me out of here, and then…we need to talk." Her look pierced Wade before she transferred and settled it on Buck. "We all need to talk."

FIFTEEN

The sheriff's office was quiet this morning. Aaliyah tugged open the door and offered a half-hearted wave to the woman at the front desk behind the plexiglass.

"Hi, Rhonda."

"Aaliyah!" Rhonda stood up quickly, hurrying around the desk to open the door, giving Aaliyah access to the back room. "Buck said you'd be laid up for days! And look at you, on crutches! You poor dear. You've been through the wringer!"

Aaliyah smirked, snapping her fingers at Peaches, who followed, her toenails clicking on the floor. "What does Buck know?" She managed to get through the doorway without banging her elbows on the doorframe as she worked the awkwardness of her crutches.

Rhonda laughed and motioned with her hand. "He's in the back." She gave Aaliyah a friendly grin and returned to her desk.

Aaliyah hesitated for a moment, adjusting her weight on her crutches. Buck and Wade had helped her from the river and driven her to the hospital. It had been a long drive. A person didn't come out from the Bob in a few minutes and reach civilization. She could tell both Wade and Buck had wanted to say something, to fill the silence, but they hadn't.

Perhaps because they knew she was in pain, and perhaps because they didn't know what to say.

Truth be told, she hadn't known what to say either. She'd waffled between anger at both men for different reasons, relief that they had found her and outright nerves that it was Gordon who had known where to find her. When would he become a part of her past? The Arrowhead Killer needed to be retired behind bars, far away from her and from any claim on her past or her future.

At the hospital, she'd let the two men hover in the waiting room of the ER. A fractured ankle later, a cast and two crutches, and she had let them help her home. The tension and unspoken words had been thick between them. Her birth father and—who was Wade to her now? They'd shared a kiss. They'd shared far more than a kiss if one were to be finicky. The amount of sheer life they'd lived in the last two weeks was enough to thrust two people together, but so were the secrets that had been unveiled. Wade was responsible for that, and his process of unveiling felt deceptive. But was that fair? To Wade? Just because Buck and Gordon and even her parents had been deceptive in their own ways, did that mean Wade had been too, or had he been attempting to be tactful? Careful. It was his job, after all. And the other nagging fact that she couldn't erase from her mind was that all of them—with the exception of Gordon—seemed to have harbored secrets for the same reason: to protect her.

Conflicted, Aaliyah made her way through the maze of desks to the office in the back. Buck's office. She stopped in the doorway, studying the man for a minute. Her godfather. Her *birth father*.

"Aaliyah!" He stood up quickly, his coffee sloshing over the side of his mug onto his desk. "Come in!" He shot a

glance at the corner of the room, and everything in Aaliyah stilled.

Wade Marlowe sat in the corner. Aaliyah hadn't expected him to be there, to be balancing a to-go cup of coffee on his knee that was crossed over his leg. She hadn't
expected their eyes to meet and for a zillion unspoken questions to pass between them in a split second.

"Wade."

"Hey," he answered, tipping his head toward her foot.
"How's the ankle?"

"It's—good." Now what? She'd wanted to come in con-
fident. She had intended to tell Buck it was time they talked
since they hadn't seen one another since the hospital. She
had questions. She needed answers. But instead, Wade was
here too, and she wasn't sure how to handle them both at
the same time.

Besides, Wade looked serious. His dark eyes had a storm
brewing in them that waned only a little when she walked
in.

Buck shifted and addressed him. "Well, I guess we can
chat later," he said congenially to Wade.

Wade gave him a thin smile. "Or we can chat now. I
think Aaliyah deserves to hear what you have to say as
much as I do."

Buck's shoulders sagged in defeat. He slumped down
onto his chair and waved Aaliyah toward the other empty
chair in the room. "Have a seat, I guess."

She almost felt bad for Buck as she took her seat. But she
could sense there was more—even more than she thought
she knew—and the expression on Wade's face only confirmed that.

"So...you're my father?" She finally worked up the nerve
to ask, thankful that Peaches had sat on the floor next to

her. She was happy to sink her hand into the dog's fur for comfort and support.

Buck cleared his throat, his hands folded and resting on the desk in front of him. He tapped his thumbs together. A lift of his hazel eyes met hers, and Aaliyah could see the resemblance to herself in him. Now that she looked at the sheriff through fresh eyes and a new story, she could see that she was a part of Buck.

"What happened?" Aaliyah was willing to hear him out. They could choose to get lost in the wilderness of unknowns and secrets, or they could face the wild of them and see what happened.

Buck glanced at Wade and then Aaliyah before settling his attention on his folded hands. He cleared his throat. "I met Deborah when she came into Park Springs twenty-five years ago. I didn't know much about her, but…" he had the decency to look sheepish "…one night, one thing led to another. When I found out Deborah was pregnant—with you—" Buck lifted his eyes and then dropped them as if addressing Aaliyah directly was too painful "—I panicked. I was a law enforcement officer at the time. I didn't know how it would look. Deborah wasn't—she lived in the shelter. It would look like I'd taken advantage of her."

Understanding dawned on Aaliyah, although she had a tough time finding sympathy for Buck.

He reached for a pen lying on his desk and began to twirl it between his thumb and index finger.

Wade shifted on his chair, leaning forward. "So you abandoned Deborah to figure it out on her own."

Buck winced and flipped the pen away from him. He leaned back in his chair and closed his eyes. "I'm not proud of it. I'm not proud of what I did."

Aaliyah fought back hot tears that sprang to her eyes.

"So when I was found behind the church and Deborah had disappeared, you didn't put it all together in your mind? You didn't think maybe I was your child and maybe the dead woman was Deborah?" She tasted a surge of bitterness on her tongue.

Buck met her accusing stare straight on. "Sure, I questioned it. But you were found, and it was two months later Deborah's body was discovered in the wilderness. And—without going into the graphic details—she wasn't recognizable at the time. You know that. We had no way of identifying her."

Wade interrupted with his conclusion. "So you assumed that Deborah had left town pregnant with your baby, and that Aaliyah, as an infant, was someone totally unrelated?"

Buck's jaw worked back and forth as if to squelch emotion. "Except the baby had red hair—like my mother's." The words came out hoarse, and he looked to the ceiling. "I had a feeling, just no way to prove it. But that's why I arranged for your parents, Aaliyah, to take you in. It kept you close, and I—could be near you. Just in case."

"And it gave Gordon a wide-open door to continue what he was doing for the next twenty-five years," Aaliyah concluded.

Buck shifted his eyes between Wade and Aaliyah. "I had no idea about Gordon. Charlie Beedle was a suspect because of the arrowhead bracelets. It seemed plausible to me. Not to mention, Deborah had said she was going to leave town. That body could have been anyone, and the baby—"

"It wouldn't have been hard to put the pieces together with some honesty on your part." Wade's conclusion was the elephant in the room.

But in that moment, something else became remarkably clear to Aaliyah. She breathed a prayer for the strength to communicate it, because she also didn't want to validate Buck's actions. He was a sheriff. He had been in law enforcement for years. His irresponsibility and his cowardice had enabled a string of horrific events through Gordon.

And yet…

Aaliyah took a step toward Buck. He eyed her with resignation and guilt. She reached across the desk and laid her palm over his hand.

God, give me the ability to say what needs to be said.

"What you did, to Deborah, was…" She struggled to find the words. "Wrong." There was no other word for it. "But I also believe—because I know you, Buck—that when you wondered if I was yours, you also kept that to yourself because—" She swallowed back a lump that grew in her throat.

A tear trailed down Buck's weathered cheek.

Aaliyah blinked rapidly to keep her own from falling. "Because you were looking out for me. In your way. You were protecting me."

"I never meant to abandon you, Aaliyah." Buck's chest caught in a stifled sob of remorse. He turned his hand so he could grasp hers. "I was wrong."

Those words were more healing than Aaliyah could imagine. There would be much more healing that needed to come yet. But for now—and for the first time—she believed she knew the full truth.

The office door burst open and hit the wall. Wade's head shot up in surprise, and Aaliyah spun around just as her parents rushed through the door. She'd seen them last night in the hospital and told them this morning she was going to confront Buck. She'd not expected them to follow.

Her mother enveloped her in her arms without asking,

without hesitating. Her father embraced them both, and they stood in a circle in Buck's office.

"We decided we couldn't let you and Buck try to carry this alone. We were a part of it too. In a way, our silence was to protect you but—we're so sorry we weren't honest with you about everything!" Aaliyah's mother wept.

"You're safe now." Her father's voice was rough with emotion. "We can all start over."

Start over.

It was too simple really, but yet, wasn't that grace too? And being abandoned—well, Aaliyah was beginning to see that her abandonment was, in a strange way, out of love. And her parents hadn't abandoned her, but in their own way—right or wrong—had tried to protect her. As had Buck. As had Wade.

She turned to bring Wade into the circle.

Buck gave her a small smile, but Aaliyah searched beyond him, scanning the room.

Wade was gone.

Aaliyah poured a cup of coffee into a pottery mug of bright orange. Today had been an emotional one. So many pieces had come together with a mixture of healing, wounding, and yes, even scarring.

She set the mug on the counter and, with the assistance of her crutches, crouched down to eye level with Peaches, who was at her side.

"And you, sweet girl." Aaliyah pressed her forehead to the dog's before pulling back and planting a kiss on Peaches's head. "You are the best dog in the entire world." Sure, most dog owners said that about their dogs, but she was pretty convinced there wasn't a better dog should Peaches be put up to the test.

Aaliyah raised her head at the knock on her door.

Boosting herself up with the crutches, she left her coffee behind and moved to answer it. She'd been hoping for the first quiet evening at home for some time. She needed to be able to sit back and process all that had happened. She needed to be able to segment her feelings and figure out the best way to move forward—in her relationship with her parents and with her birth father, Buck.

Pulling the door open, her heart flipped.

Wade Marlowe stood on the stoop, a day's worth of dark stubble on his face, his dark hair mussed from a fresh shower, and his coffee-colored eyes matching the brew he held in his hands. Two cups. He smiled sheepishly.

"Guess you can't take this." He lifted one of the to-go cups and motioned toward her crutches.

Aaliyah squelched the nervous twist to her stomach. She managed a small smile. "I'll still drink it." She nodded toward a side table. "You can set it there."

Wade followed her instruction.

"Umm, did you want to come in?"

"Actually," Wade shifted his weight onto his other foot, "I was going to let you know I'm going to be heading back to Helena."

"Oh." Aaliyah squelched the sinking sensation in her stomach. It was probably for the best. "Well…thank you." She guessed. Her gratitude came out stilted.

Thank you for finding my birth mother.
Thank you for revealing the painful secrets of my past.
Thank you for saving me from a serial killer.
Thank you for upending my life…

What could she say? There was such a mixture of emotion when it came to Wade Marlowe.

"I hope everything can get worked out between you and

your family." Wade lifted his coffee in a casual farewell laden with unspoken words.

Aaliyah nodded. "Thanks."

"Well." Wade took a deep breath. "You take care."

"I will, thanks." Aaliyah didn't know what else to say. They had met under extreme circumstances. Kissed under the darkest of moments. Explored friendship while warding off chaos and impending death.

Wade turned his back and started down the walk toward his vehicle. Aaliyah watched him, holding on to her crutches tighter than was necessary. She was going to let him go. She was going to let him walk away. She had to, didn't she? He had, in a way, sided with Buck in Buck's deceit. He had known that she was Buck's daughter, and yet he'd said nothing. He had—

Protector.

That was the word that came to mind and drowned out all of Aaliyah's excuses.

Wade Marlowe was a protector. He wasn't perfect, but he had done everything, including risk his life, to make sure hers could continue. Wade was the epitome of what she, Aaliyah Terrence, wanted in her life. Someone who, regardless of circumstances, would stand behind her. Like a lion behind a lioness.

Aaliyah made her decision. She shouted, "Wade! Wait!"

He turned, question in his eyes.

Aaliyah's words stuck in her throat.

They stared at each other.

"I'm sorry," she said without embellishing or explaining.

Wade's brows furrowed. "What for?"

"For doubting your honesty. For running away after you risked your life to save me."

"I don't blame you for that." Wade took a step back up the walk toward her. "You had every right to be upset."

"But not to blame you." Aaliyah sucked in a steadying breath. She worked her crutches forward so she could step out of her door onto the front stoop. "You protected me. You fought for me. You—hardly knew me, but you…cared."

Wade's Adam's apple bobbed as he swallowed hard. He looked down at his coffee and then bent to set it on the sidewalk. When he straightened, he closed the distance between them. His eyes burrowed into Aaliyah's. "I care. I care more than I thought I would care. I never wanted to make you feel like I was damaging your life—damaging who you were."

"I know," Aaliyah breathed. She could smell his cologne, spicy, warm…safe.

"I only ever wanted to fight for you—on your behalf—but I had to make a call, and maybe I didn't make the right one." Wade seemed to struggle, scowling at himself as though his internal thoughts were warring to make sense of things.

Aaliyah leaned against a crutch and lifted her hand from the other one just enough to trace along Wade's hairline at his temple. "Your sister would be proud of you."

Wade's eyes glistened with emotion, and Aaliyah offered him a watery smile. "The fact is we're all a little bit abandoned, by someone. Whether by their choice or their death or their will. But, when you really care, you fight for them. I see that now. And I want to believe Deborah fought for me when she left me behind instead of in Gordon's care. I believe Buck—in his own way—fought for me and has spent his life watching over me. My parents? They've never not believed in me."

Wade turned his face so her hand palmed his cheek. His eyes stayed locked with hers. "I have to go back to Helena, to close the case." He took a step onto the stoop and looked down at her now, reaching forward to help her balance with her broken ankle. "I'd like to come back to Park Springs. I'd like to come back to you."

Aaliyah could only smile then. She had no more words, and she hoped that Wade could read her eyes.

He did.

He closed the distance between them, his lips softly brushing hers. "I know it's fast, I know we have a ways to go, but I think I'm falling in love with you." Wade spoke the words against her mouth, his lips featherlight against hers.

It was what her heart wanted to hear. What her heart ached to hear. Aaliyah responded by pressing her lips against Wade's, deepening the kiss and the promise.

"Well, well!" A deep, wobbly voice interrupted their moment.

Wade and Aaliyah drew back, Wade not loosening his grip on her waist.

Charlie Beedle stood on the walk behind Wade, a loaf of fresh-baked bread in his hands. His eyes twinkled, his hat cocked to the side of his head. He chuckled. "I was just bringin' over some bread, but you two get on with your kissin'. I'll just leave it here." He set the bread on the walk next to Wade's coffee.

Wade's chuckle joined Aaliyah's soft laughter.

Charlie lifted his hand in a wave, oblivious to the journey they had been on the last couple of weeks. He wobbled back toward his house, and Wade turned back to Aaliyah.

"Here's to hope," he whispered.

"Here's to us," she replied.

And somehow, deep in Aaliyah's heart, she knew that her story had only just begun.

* * * * *

Dear Reader,

What a joy to write a story that centers around belonging and protection. As an adoptee myself, there are so many emotions of abandonment and so many questions that swirl in my mind. But then, there are also the truths. That every child is loved, if by no one else than THE PROTECTOR. Our Heavenly Father. We all have journeys of brokenness to travel. Regrets, the need for redemption, and most of all, the story of adoption. Because all of us who have come to the Lord have experienced this adoption and this protection.

It's a beautiful journey. Even in the chaos.

I pray you'll find blessing in your darkness and refuge in your storms.

Jaime Jo